DAISY'S DARKNESS

WHEELS & HOGS GARAGE
BOOK 6

D.M. EARL

Copyright @ 2021 D. M. Earl
Published by D. M. Earl

All rights reserved. Except for use in any review, the reproduction or utilization of this work in whole or in any part in any form by any electronic, mechanical or any other means, now or hereafter invented including photocopying, recording, information storage and retrieval systems-except in the case of brief quotations embodied in the critical article or reviews-without permission in writing from the author. This book may not be resold or redistributed without the express consent of the author.

For any questions or comments please email the author directly at DM@DMEARL.COM

This book is a work of fiction. All characters, events and places portrayed in this book are products of the author's imagination and are either fictitious or are used fictitiously. Any similarity to real persons, living or deceased is purely coincidental and not intentional.

This book contains sexual encounters, consensual and graphic language that some readers may find objectionable. It contains graphic material that is not suitable for anyone under the age of 18.

Romantic Erotic Mature Audience.

ACKNOWLEDGMENTS

My Phenomenal Team of Karen Hrdlicka, JoAnna Walker@Just Write Creations & Katie Harder-Schauer y'all are my lifeline. Thank you for always making time for my babies and taking such good care of each manuscript from beginning to end. I am forever in your debt.

Enticing Journey Book Promotions Ena & Amanda handle all my book promotions from beginning to end and have become a very important part of my Indie team. Thank you for what you do which allows me to do I want...to write.

Bloggers for sharing my new releases and for just getting my name out there. Humbled thanks.

My Horde Readers Group y'all hold me up and give me the push to keep going no matter what. I thank each of you for your continued support.

My hubby Chuck who has supported me from the beginning. Thanks for letting me live my dream."

I dedicate this book to every person young and old who have had to endure and struggle with any of the subjects this book touches on. Remember you are not ALONE, reach out for HELP and never lose HOPE.

To my beautiful niece Haley, I'm humbled and grateful each and every day for being a part of your life honey. From the moment you were born and every day since to be able to watch you grow and become the young woman you are today is priceless. Words that come to mind are proud, honored and inspired to name just a few. Thank you for allowing to be part of your life and for bringing sunshine into mine."

DAISY'S DIARY

My Thoughts

June 15

Yay, last day of school. I'm free for the summer. Well kind of, Mom has all these projects for both of us to bond, whatever that means, but still gonna hang with my queens and just chill. Maybe get some stuff done, draw, and hang out. Can't wait.

June 17

Oh my God, you won't believe who Jagger is... dating. Never...you will you believe it. Sabrina. WTF, Big Brother...This is totally going to ruin my summer. I'm on my way to HELL. She is one of "those girls" and that means if they are together she will be at my house. My world is so over as I know it.

June 18

Thank God I have friends. Had to get out of the

house. Everything seems to be *closing in* on me lately. Even when I'm talking to or hanging with my queens- Akiria, V, Amethyst, or Bird they don't even seem to get me. What's going on? I can't talk to my mom because I don't want to disappoint her or even know how to explain my feelings of nothingness.

June 29

Sorry haven't checked in. Life is getting weird. Jagger is still with the bitch. Why can't he see what a horrible person she is or how mean she is? Even when we were in middle school everyone knew to stay away from Sabrina. The queens and I have talked about it and seems Sabrina gives it away, if you know what I mean. And Jagger has been pretty happy, even to the point of whistling. Just yuck! Can't even think about that WTF, Big Brother!!! You have really low standards. And like Archie always says, why buy the cow when the milk is free?

July 4

Wow, how did I not know Cadence's little brother, Griffin, was so smoking' hot? Damn, he was at the annual Wheels & Hogs BBQ alone (Yay me) even said hi and spoke to me for a couple of minutes. He is cute-funny-quiet and seems real. That's all for now. Had a good day.

July 10

Been spending time with Mom at the garage. They're all totally nuts. And they keep acting like I'm still a kid. Like I don't hear or say swear words. What's with grown men saying dang or heck around me 'cause I have a vagina? Really, like damn and hell will burn my ears. They should hear how we all talk and text each other. Text especially, hahahah. Then we would see who'd be blushing. Some of the sex texts and jokes that Amethyst sends crack me up. She really finds the good ones. Wish we could all get together more but seems like everyone is doing their own thing. Whatever!

July 12

That bitch (oops better never let Mom hear me) Jagger is dating is getting on my last nerve. Every time she's around, the bitch is knocking into me and she even pushed me hard to watch me fall down. I banged my damn hip and elbow 'cause of her. Well, that's kinda easy as I'm a klutz, but who does she think she is? And today as she walked into the house while I was leaving, she grabbed my upper arm hard. I'm sure that shit will leave a bruise. She's such a tramp and I wanted to tell Jagger, but he seems so happy. I'll just have to avoid her in my own house. Not to mention she called me out for eating a donut. "Daisy, you shouldn't wear that type of blouse, it shows your donut roll." Really? Whatever, bitch. Keep it up I'll show you my fist.

July 14

Holy crap, what a day. The queens and I went to the mall today. As always, we got split up because they all have their favorite stores and I just kept moving on. I was in the baby store, trying to get something for Hope, when someone pushed me from behind. It was Sabrina and her mean *biotch* clique. Then they started pushing me back and forth and I actually got frightened. No one did anything. Before they left, Sabrina got in my face and told me I better spoil Trinity's brat 'cause no guy would want to f**k me because I'm so ugly and fat. I didn't tell anyone about this. Maybe she's right. Got to watch what I'm eating, don't want to start high school as one of the "fat girls."

July 15

Shitty day don't even want to go into it. Had words with everyone in my life. Why won't they just leave me the hell alone? I hate being around anyone right now.

July 17

Got to spend the day at Cadence and Trinity's place. I played with Hope most of the day to give Trinity a break. God, I love that little girl. She is so cute and is getting her own little diva/queen personality. And she likes, no loves, me no matter what. And to top the day off, Griffin stopped by and even stayed for dinner. We all played board games after and hung out. I know he is like Jagger's age or older, but when we talk, it's like he is the only one that truly gets me. He actually listens to what I have to say. Well anyway, tired but had a great day.

July 19

Mom doesn't understand me at all. She wants me to be how she wants me to be and that's it. She won't listen to me anymore. Tries to treat me like a frigging kid. I'm not her baby anymore. She got pissed because I have a Facebook page and don't want to friend her. Why would I? She doesn't have to be in all my business all the time just because she's my mom, does she? And I have been eating less and lost 3 lbs. Awesome. Going to keep going. I won't be fat in high school, no matter what I have to do.

July 23

Man it's gross. Mom and Des think I don't know what the googly eyes and all that kissy face shit and touching means. I might only be a teenager but I do know about sex. They talked about it in junior high. And Mom had 'the talk' with me too. Gross, what's so great about it? I know girls who have gone all the way, but totally yuck. But...if Griffin wanted to kiss me maybe I'd let him. Just kiss though or maybe more. Damn it, now I'm so confused. And he's so cute. Nite.

July 24

I'm getting sick of these Sunday family meals. Everyone from Wheels & Hogs is now my "family." I don't get a choice, it just is. Today it's at Ann's cabin behind the garage. She is the grandma of the kids Gabriel and Fern are raising. Emma and Charlie split their time between Ann's and the Murphys' home. Lydia was Fern's friend who passed away from cancer. She wanted all three adults to raise her kids. Now this is a perfect example, these people aren't even part of Wheels & Hogs but now have become part of the "family." Sick of all this crap. Just wanted to stay home, listen to my music and chill. And how can I diet with everyone watching me, forcing me to eat something. "Daisy try this" or "Daisy a little of this." Makes me so frigging mad. Was checking out Facebook and someone was talking about some girl who cuts. Didn't really know what that is so I went online to check it out. Not that I would do that but they say it helps relieve pressure and stress. I need to find something that does that for me. Got to go, Mom is calling. Later.

July 25

Dang it, I can't get a break. I came home from Bird's house today to find Jagger and Sabrina were in his room. And from the sounds of it, going at it like rabbits. They're having sex, or something close I think. YUCK. What is wrong with my brother? With all the girls out there, he picks the Wicked Bitch of the West. Laughing out loud I crack myself up. Well, tried to ignore them, went into the kitchen to get some carrots and turned around to find Sabrina watching me. And the look in her eyes scared me. As I walked past her, she pinched my arm and I let out a yelp. She smiled and went to get something to drink. Why me? What did I do to her that she hates me so much? God, what have I ever done that you keep making my life so hard? Mom always says have faith. It's getting harder and harder. Time for some music.

July 28

Well, thought today would be a good day, but of course Jagger's *biotch* was at our house again. As usual

I get the brunt of her hate. She pushed me and I fell down, scraping both knees. She was gone before Mom and Des got home. Des was going to BBQ hot dogs and hamburgers (real healthy) and I was helping Mom cut up stuff in the kitchen. I accidentally cut my thumb while slicing tomatoes. At first, I just watched it bleed, 'cause for some reason it fascinated me. My body seemed to relax as the blood flowed out of my finger. Then of course when Mom saw it, she started to freak—screaming and going all crazy. Then she pulled me to the sink, putting my injured thumb under cold water. That hurt like hell. Then she wrapped it in a towel so she could get some gauze and tape. Later in bed, I unwrapped it and squeezed it really hard. It started to bleed and once again I was fascinated. Watching my blood, it felt like all the pressure inside my head and body was released as the blood flowed. Relax, I'm not a cutter...I'm not going to do that, but just saying I can kind of see why some people do it.

July 30

Last of the summer parties at Bird's house. All the queens were there and we had a blast. All of us girls out in the sun all day, swimming and hanging. Her dad BBQ'd some chicken, brats, and hot dogs. Bird's parents seem nice, but I think like all parents when it's your kid the kid thinks differently. Anyway, one of my best days of summer vacation. Mom wants to take a weekend and go somewhere. Don't want to hurt her feelings, don't want to go anywhere. Especially with her and Des. We'll see, don't really have a say in my own life right now.

August 4

Sorry haven't felt much like writing. Good news lost another 8 lbs., total of I think 13 lbs. so far. Mom and Des say I'm too skinny but is that even possible? NOT. I found a way to make sure I don't gain a ton of weight when I eat. Binge and then purge. Yeah, sounds gross, I get it, but if you just do it when you eat something, you shouldn't gain weight, it works. When I was at Bird's house, her mom made some awesome desserts and I wanted them but didn't want to gain any weight back, so I went in her bathroom and made myself sick. Got caught by her mom but just told her I ate way too much and wasn't feeling well. Think she believed me. Really don't care if she didn't as she isn't friends with my mom, so no worries. Anyway, that's it for now.

August 8

Sabrina was again at my house. What the ever-lovin' fuck. Doesn't she have a home? And to make it worse, Jagger was in the garage working on his bike. Guess with who???? Yep, Griffin. Thought this was perfect until I saw the gleam in Sabrina's eye. Not catching on, I went to get drinks and she followed me, pinching my arm again. Damn, that hurt like a bitch. I turned and she literally pushed me down to my ass. Told me that Griffin would never be into a "gross bitch" like me. Right when I was going to reply back, I heard the doorbell. Sabrina goes to open it like it's her own house. I walk into the hallway to see one of her mean girls, Heather, walk in. They both turn to me and smile. Then they turn and walk out to the garage.

By the time I get drinks and head out, I almost drop them when I see Heather hanging on Griffin. I think my heart broke a bit. And to make it worse, no one noticed except Sabrina. Who just smiled at me like a cat who caught her prey. Whores.

August 12

Lost another 2.5 lbs. so at 15.5 lbs. gone. Doesn't matter anymore. Nothing really does. Feel so alone and lonely. Even with my queens, missing that usual closeness since I'm not sharing everything with them. They know something is up but I'm not letting them in. I did something tonight. Looked it up online and then I took one of the knives from Mom's butcher block and cut my inner thigh. A very small cut, but wow, when the blood started to come out, the pain in my soul felt like it flowed with my blood. And some of that pain is because of what Jagger said earlier. Heather and Griffin are together. Guess Sabrina was right, why would such a hot guy like Griffin want a fat ass like me. Anyhow got to get some exercising in later.

August 17

Well, I at least got this weight loss thing down. Lost 4 lbs. so almost at 20 lbs. Mom is starting to freak out, as usual. Even made a doctor's appointment for me. And Des is watching me constantly. I know they don't think this is normal teenager girl shit, but I feel so disconnected from them, nope, from everyone in my life. Like I live in the house with a bunch of strangers, but I'm not part of any of the crap that goes down. Don't even want to see Archie or Willow and that's a first. Those two usually crack me up, not to mention they always bring my spirits up. Haven't stopped by to check on Trinity either. I do miss lil' diva Hope. Maybe tomorrow. Lately I'm so tired all the time. No energy, which is fuckin' crazy 'cause I weigh less.

August 19

Mom took me for school clothes today. Couldn't hide anymore how much weight I lost. She couldn't believe it. I don't think she's mad, just worried. Anyhow even though I hate it, a part of me missed being with her. She's my mom. She's my constant. I have always been able to go to her and tell her everything and anything. Not to mention my periods have been really off. I looked online and it said since I've lost weight that could be causing it. Who cares anyway? No boys are into me at all. I'm just the ugly-fat-nerdy girl.

August 21

Today V called me. Somehow, she figured out some of the things I've been doing. She shared with me that she spent some time in the hospital this summer and was seeing a therapist. I said why and all she told me was that life was hard especially for teenage girls. Or that is what her counselor told her. She said that if I needed to talk to someone, she was always there for me.

I hung up and broke out sobbing like a baby. Why can't I reach out to anyone to help me? I feel like I'm on a one-way ride that will end when there is nothing left of me. I feel so empty and useless. I've been cutting a bit more, not deep or long cuts, just enough to bleed. I need, no crave, the feeling I get watching the blood run out. In my head I know this is so wrong, but the way it makes me feel I can't stop. Not now at least. Maybe when things get better, who knows.

August 28

First day of high school. Yay. NOT. Went ok, the queens and I are all together which is good. And I didn't see Sabrina but what I saw was worse. Heather. That's Heather and Griffin together, hand in hand in the halls at school. When she saw me watching them, she just squinted her eyes and then smiled. Totally broke my heart. I thought he would be different. He was always really nice to me, said hi whenever he saw me, and would even talk to me. He didn't today when they walked past. Life sucks. And now I hate Heather along with Sabrina. Hope they both die a painful death. Too bad I don't know how to put a curse on someone 'cause I would.

August 31

I'm in all advanced classes as are Bird, V, Arikia, and Amethyst. This is good because none of Sabrina and her mean girl squad are. They are way too stupid. Yeah, that is mean but whatever. Since the first day I have been pushed, pinched, and made fun of by all of them. It's like they are on a mission to hurt me, no matter what. And they find me no matter where I go. Well, hopefully they move on from me soon. There has got to be a bigger loser in this school than me. That is their MO anyway. Find someone to pick on, drag them down, then find another loser.

September 5

Labor Day, yay first day off. BBQ of course at our house. The Horde and bikers all came. Also Sabrina and Heather. What tramps. They were all over Bear and Ugly (the bikers). And poor Griffin, I even felt sorry for him. Heather treats him like crap. Don't think it's going to last. I overheard Griffin tell Jagger that even though he is getting some regularly (totally gross) that it wasn't worth the hassle. I secretly hope he dumps her. Everyone was surprised at the weight I had lost. Trinity was starting to show. And lil' Hope is growing up so frigging fast. She was putting sentences together kind of but she was so cute. Spent most of my time playing with her and her dolls. What I wouldn't give to be a kid again. Literally had no pressure back then.

September 13

Sorry, haven't had time or energy to put my thoughts down. School is kicking my butt, as is Sabrina. Plus, something is going on with my queens. Everyone seems to be going in different directions and we aren't connecting at all. Feel so lost, I have no one. I know V isn't as close to her mom but she is tight with her dad. Amethyst was cool with both of her parents. Arikia had, I guess you would call it, a unique relationship with her mom. Her mom didn't want her to dress down but dress to show her figure. You got it flaunt it, I guess. Bird seems cool with her parents. She's the only one among us whose family is into their faith. If it works, good for them. The way I'm feeling God ain't doing me no favors. Mom loves me, I know this, but lately I'm having nightmares about Jagger and my dad. He was a son of a bitch as Mom says, but there were some good times. But since the dreams, every time someone yells or gets mad I just totally panic. My head is so fucked up right now.

September 24

Damn it. Almost cut too deep this time. Couldn't stop the bleeding. Started freakin' out, thought I nicked something, like a vein. Finally, I put ice on it and looked up on the Internet how to stop bleeding. It said Vaseline helps stop bleeding so I put a bunch on and it eventually stopped. But as weird as this sounds, watching myself bleed releases all the pressures in my head. The ugly stuff goes away and I feel "normal" for a bit. Whatever normal is. I almost had to tell Mom, who would have freaked out if she saw all the little scars on my upper and inner thighs. Let alone under my arms by my armpits. Places no one sees. I even tried the bottom of my foot but that made walking difficult. DUH.

October 4

Besides school, been staying in my room a lot by

myself. Jagger and the *Biotch* are still hanging together, so even my own house isn't safe. She actually pushed me down again the other day in the hallway, the horse-face that she is. Banged my head into the baseboard and had a goose egg on my forehead. Des saw it and I told him I fell, just didn't mention who pushed me. My life totally SUCKS. School is so hard with so much homework, plus my chores and my main problem, Sabrina. Why does this chick hate me so much? I've never done anything to her. And it's getting worse. I can't cut under my arms any longer due to all the bruising from her pinching, slapping, and punching me. And having to cover that crap up. Jagger seems to be pulling back from her. In the bathroom the other day at school, V was in a stall and heard Sabrina bitching about Jagger seeming like he's not wanting to hang with her as much. She was gonna pull out all the stops, whatever the hell that means.

October 7

Going to the movies with the queens. Yeah. Mom wants me home by 11:00 p.m. What the hell? I'm not a baby anymore. Will just get home late and tell her we got caught by a train or something. Can't wait to get out and do something fun for a change.

October 9

Well, grounded for two weeks because I got home at 12:15a.m. and was way late. Mom didn't buy it and Des actually stuck up for me. Mom told him to mind his business. So then they fought. Guess I can't do anything right.

October 11

Well, damn close call. I was in my room, forgot to lock the damn door, and Jagger came in when I was just about to cut myself. I made up some sad story and he believed it, I think. But he's watching me all the time now. Especially when we eat. I have lost about 25 lbs. now, so it's like they think I'm starving myself. Crap, I could lose another 25 lbs. and still have more to go. Whatever, it's my body and the only thing I can control in my messed up life. At least my body 'cause my mind is gone. I thought I saw my dad the other day at the mall. Scared the shit out of me. Didn't mention to Mom or Des. Praying it was just my mind playing games as it has been. Think I'm going crazy.

October 13

Well, Mom is totally pissed at me. I failed one of my tests and didn't finish a project. She wants to talk to my counselor at school. WTF for? They don't care. And with the holidays just around the corner, I wish I could go away until they were over. Hate my life and everyone in it. Why can't they mind their business for Christ's sake?

October 14

Mom is such a raging nosy bitch. In my business all the time. HATE IT and HER!

October 18

Trinity called to see if I wanted to go trick-or-treating with her and Hope. I would need a costume though. I love that little girl and Trinity is so cool. Said I would and I'll figure something out. School sucks and so does this house. And Sabrina's still here all the time during the day but manages to leave before Mom gets home. And she is as mean as ever. The other day, she hit me from behind in the back of my head. Hard. Never thought my life would be like this. In my own house. I am always sad. Why am I always so sad?

October 23

Mom and her stupid Sunday dinners. Tonight, it was all of us with Gabriel, Fern, and the kids. Emma and Charlie are cute but a handful. Older than Hope so they want constant attention. I was so overwhelmed I actually spilled Gabriel's coffee on my hand just to get out of the rest of the night. Does that make me a lunatic? Hurting myself to get out of spending quality time with my family. Not sure but thinking it is leaning that way. Crazy Daisy.

October 25

My nosy counselor at school told Mom that my grades are failing and that they think something is going on. Then she asked if something was going on in our home. Was there someone there who might be touching me inappropriately, like maybe Des. She said since he isn't my father maybe I was afraid to say something and wanted us to know that it was a safe place. Thought Mom was going to put the chick in the damn hospital. Well, good news, last time we speak to my counselor;

bad news, Mom is looking for a therapist who deals with teenagers. Just great. And I haven't lost a pound of weight in six days. Something is wrong. I'm vomiting more and not losing. Something is totally wrong.

October 29

My Halloween costume was a zombie until Mom put the kibosh on it. Said it would scare Hope. So now I'm going as a plain old ghost with a sheet. Easy-peasy.

October 31

Man, was tonight fun. Trinity let me bring my queens with so Bird was Phantom of the Opera, V was some kind of Chinese something, Arikia was like Goth Girl, and Amethyst was a baby. Hope was so excited and even Cadence and guess who...Yeah, Griffin showed up and went with us. WE all had a blast 'cause Cadence is so damn funny. Sometimes it's hard to believe Cadence and Trinity had such messed-up lives because they seem to get along awesome together. And Hope just completes them. Trinity was getting tired fast though. So after my queens left, it was just Cadence, Griffin, and me helping Hope go through her candy. I gave her all her favorites from my stash. She literally threw herself into my arms screaming and laughing.

"Daisy, I luv u so much. Tanks for goong with uds. You made a good ghost too."

My heart was so full because of that little girl. One of my best nights too. Until I was getting ready to leave and Griffin walked me down to Mom's car. He wanted to know if I was ok. I looked up at him for a bit then just shook my head and left. Why does he care now? He has Heather and is *gettin' some*, right? Nothing ever goes right in my life.

November 6

School is killing me. I am doing homework until at least midnight most nights. Don't these teachers like us? What happened to enjoy your teen years? I despise mine so far, for fuck's sake.

November 10

Mom reamed me today. She had reason. After school I was supposed to straighten up the house for the weekend but instead binged and vomited. Then kind of fell asleep listening to my iPod. That's where she found me. And I haven't showered in a couple of days so I know I looked like crap. Well, now I'm stuck in the house for the weekend and have to clean it tomorrow. Kill me now. PLEASE.

November 13

Sucks.

November 14

Sucks more.

November 16

Can't wait until Thanksgiving break. Time to chill.

November 19

Today I even pissed myself off. Didn't interact with the family all day and when Mom said dinner was ready, told her I wasn't eating, didn't feel good. Went in the kitchen later and she had made all my favorites. I'm such a brat. WHY?

November 22

Managed to blow off the therapist appointment today because of school. I know I'm a huge disappointment to my mom, but don't need someone picking through my head. And Sabrina is the Devil reincarnated. I've got bruises all over.

November 23

Well, I did it now. At Gabriel and Fern's for Turkey Day and I blew up at my mom in front of everyone. I know they are all worried but give me some space. I'm not a kid any longer. Really. Then Mom and Des pulled me into a bedroom to give me shit. I felt like I was 5 years old. Whatever. I didn't eat a lot and even puked in the bathroom there. Lost 2 lbs. so that's good. Looks like I'm back on track. Yay me!!

November 30

I'm going to take a break from writing in my diary. I need a break from everything. Especially my own life. Nothing I do seems like enough.

December 18

The wedding of Cadence and Trinity is coming along. Can't believe they are tying the knot on New Year's Eve. Pretty romantic.

December 24

Went to Wolf's house. What a surprise, it was gorgeous. Wolf and Willow kissed under mistletoe. Me, I sat in a corner most of the night. Alone and lonely.

December 25

Glad this is over. Santa came this morning, well Bear in a Santa suit. Cute though for Charlie, Emma, and Hope. Guess most would have considered it a nice day. I thought it was okay. We surprised Mom with her gift of a new laptop. Kind of felt like old times for a tiny bit. Still don't understand how I can feel so alone and lost with everyone around me. I cut two strips into my thigh after everyone went to bed. That made my Christmas better. Sick in the head ain't I?

December 31

Wow, what a day. The wedding was beautiful. And Griffin was there with Trinity, Cadence, and Hope. For a minute I thought one of my secrets was out. Trinity saw the bruises on my arm. Then later caught Sabrina squeezing the same arm, smiling as I grimaced in pain. Finally, Jagger caught her bullying me and broke up with her on the spot. I'm happy he finally saw her for what she is but know this means after Christmas break I'm going to be in some deep shit with her, because I'm sure she will turn their breakup into my fault. I don't care, today was beautiful and made my heart happy for the first time in a long time. It showed me that even though I feel lost and alone, I'm not. Everyone's still there for me, it's just up to me to step out of my comfort zone sometimes. I'm hoping next year brings many more happy days, just like today.

January 3

Damn, don't want to go back to school and what a

way to start on the first day back. My life sucks. THEY won't leave me alone. I ended up in the ER today. Mom and Des can never find out what's going on. Especially Jagger can't ever know; don't ever want to cause him any guilt and there's nothing he's responsible for. He can't help his ex-girlfriend is a total crazy-ass *biotch*.

PROLOGUE

Damn it, why do I let all this crap bring me down? I can't seem to reach the light no matter what I do. Winter break has had good and bad times. But just knowing tomorrow is time to go back to school is giving me huge frigging anxiety.

Mom and Des have tried really hard to just let me be. Like tonight at dinner, it must have showed on my face how much stress I was carrying because neither of them said one negative word. Not about my appearance, which I know I look like death warmed over. Not even about the lack of food on my plate. I did put some vegetables, salad, and two slices of roast. No bread or potatoes though. Des watched me closely throughout the meal, but said not a word. And shock of all shocks, Mom didn't ride my ass either. And thank God Jagger was at work.

Now I'm in my bedroom trying to figure out what to wear tomorrow. Since my weight loss progress, most of my clothes are baggy. And yes, that's a good thing, but also not because I can't let Mom see the clothes hanging off of me or she will get up in my business yet again. I search my closet and find a pair of old jeans, way in the back. I think I wore these in seventh grade, but fingers crossed I might be able to squeeze into them. That solves the bottom half now the top remains. I can probably get away with a T-shirt and hoodie and they should be a bit baggy as no one wears skintight hoodies. I have a plan I think to myself and smile.

After getting my clothes in order, I work on my book bag and make sure everything I need for tomorrow is in there. Also have my small bottle of mouthwash, Tums, hand wipes, and Band-Aids. Gotta be prepared, no matter what. The first two in case I need to purge for whatever reason. The next one, the wipes, for not only cleaning after said purging but also if one of my cuts breaks open and starts to bleed. That is also why I have Band-Aids. You can never be too careful.

Thinking on that, gonna take a shower tonight because I'm definitely not a morning person. Especially with not being able to sleep much lately. I can be extremely tired and then I get in bed and it's like suddenly I'm wired and can't for the life of me fall to sleep. No matter what, I've counted sheep, drank warm milk, and even taken that melatonin stuff. Crazy, don't even know why I'm not able to fall asleep 'cause I'm exhausted all the time. Not to mention the constant pain I feel in all parts of my body, especially my tummy and where all my cuts are. Also thinking some of them are either infected or on the road to being infected. My life sucks big time.

CHAPTER ONE

DAISY

With winter break over, the first day back to school I knew would suck big time. Especially after Jagger broke up with Sabrina at Trinity and Cadence's wedding. The evil tramp *biotch* that she is, other people—especially my brother—saw a glimpse of at the reception, but they still don't have a clue how this is going to make going back to school a living hell for me. That might explain the constant darkness in my soul. I feel so lonely and alone all the time, with the feeling of impending doom. And my brain keeps telling me that no one can prevent whatever is about to happen.

Thank God I have my queens. If not for Bird, V, Amethyst and Akiria, I would be totally lost. We make up one of the *nerd* groups. We'll never be in the popular crowd because we all like the same things. *Dr. Who*, memes, graphic design, drawing, music, and all the other crazy stuff we are drawn to that the "normal" kids think means we are weird and strange.

With my head in the clouds, as usual, I head directly to my locker with my brain going in all directions. Not paying attention, I reach out to open the combination when I'm hit from behind hard, being shoved directly into said locker that is sticky and wet. I feel like I can't breathe and while taking a breath something burns my nostrils immediately. Trying to pull back so I can grab a tissue from my pocket, they push harder at my back and my face hits the mess. I can feel my skin start to tingle then burn and begin to panic. Why is this happening and who is behind me for God's sake?

"What's the matter, little Daisy? No one to save you? Joey, hold her still, will you? This is your welcome back to school, you stupid bitch. Did you really think I'd forgive and forget how you manipulated that situation with Jagger at the lamest ass wedding I've ever been to? Well, I didn't forget and have been waiting impatiently for school to restart so we could reconnect. Try and guess what's all over your locker. Joey likes mixing things together. This time it's a pretty simple mix. Some dish soap, ammonia, and bleach. Let her go, Joey. Awe, damn, look at your pretty clothes, Daisy. Ruined, and why, 'cause you can't mind your own business. This is just a sample of what happens when you fuck with me, ya dumb little bitch."

I look down, seeing my clothes turning colors from the bleach mixture. My jeans and T-shirt colors have been lightened and the colors are bleeding through. As much as my clothes being ruined upsets me, what's bothering me more is how badly my cheek is burning, which is causing my eyes to tear from the constant pain. Joey continues to push and hold my face hard so I can't pull back.

"Fuck, Joey, you dick, look at her face. I told you only her clothes for Christ's sake, you idiot. Damn it! Great, Joey, can't ya do one thing right? Daisy, if you go to the nurse because your face is bothering you, keep your trap shut about what happened. We wouldn't want anything worse to happen, say to your pretty face or body, would we?"

I struggle, finally pulling away when I hear voices in the distance shouting my name loudly. Sabrina turns then looks back at me, and for a moment her eyes are filled with pure hatred before she turns, grabbing Joey's hand, and they take off running down the hall. I immediately slide down to the floor, hands in my hair, trying to keep it off of my face, which feels like it is red-hot. I'm struggling to take air in as I feel an asthma attack coming on.

"Crap, Daisy, what happened? What did that friggin' *biotch* do to you?"

Looking up at V I just shake my head, which sends fiery pain to my cheeks. Bird leans down, giving me a hand up, and we start walking toward the nurse's office. Bird grabs my hand giving it a squeeze.

"Hey, you're gonna have to speak to your parents about this. It's getting out of hand, Daisy. Sabrina is bat-ass crazy and is intentionally trying to hurt you. Really hurt you bad. It's much more than a pinch or crap like that. Please promise me you'll talk to them, Daisy?"

I know that will never happen so I shrug my shoulders as we enter the nurse's office, who turns, concern filling her face immediately.

"Oh, sweetie, what happened? Let me look at you. You other girls get to your next class, I'll take care of her from here. Go on get."

They all give me their own look, then head out to continue their first day back to school. I lean back as the nurse takes my information, knowing she is going to call my mom. This day just turned into one hell of a shitshow. I don't want to involve my mom, Jagger, or even Des in this huge cluster mess. I've been hoping Sabrina would just get tired and move on to her next victim. Obviously, the powers above do not want to grant my wish. As usual my life sucks big time right now.

Watching through the glass window as Mom and Des approach, I can see how upset both of them are. Mom tries to hide it but there is no hiding with Des. The nurse walks to the front of her office greeting them. Besides a quick hello, immediately my mom walks to me pulling me close, but is very careful not to touch any of the now flaming red and blistering skin.

"Oh, my poor girl, what happened? Who did this, Daisy? You need to tell us so it doesn't happen again. I knew something was going on, I should have tried to talk to you about this before. No more, my beauty, please, sweetie, talk to me."

Not saying anything to her, I feel Des approach us at our sides. He's quietly watching us, his face is full of rage but nothing comes from his mouth. I think he is unsure of what to say at this moment, not knowing the facts. Des is that way always, even though he's not our biological father. He's the closest Jagger and I have ever had as a father figure in our lives.

The nurse explains that an accident has occurred and my cheek came into contact with a chemical mixture of what she thinks is a bleach/ammonia mixed together. With my skin being so sensitive it caused a chemical burn. Also, she lets them know my breathing is raspy and I probably need a breathing treatment because of my asthma. She suggests a visit to the ER to get checked out. She also tells them that I didn't tell her how this happened. Both Mom and Des jerk their heads, looking at me questioningly. I say nothing and just stare back. They see my mood, knowing I'm not gonna share, so they thank the school nurse and we head out to Mom's car.

Once in the back seat, I buckle up and wait. I know it's coming, and I'm not sure how I'm going to be able to handle all of their questions coming at me without revealing anything. Not sure who's going to play the good cop this time; I'm surprised when Des starts speaking softly.

"Little Queen, I know this is not what you want to

hear but I need to get it out. No one has the fuckin' right to hurt you with their words, physically lay hands on you, or any kind of mental abuse. And I mean NEVER, Daisy. This shit was done to intentionally put you in harm's way for Christ's sake. Your mom and I can't let it go on any longer 'cause not only do we both love you, but we're responsible to make sure no harm comes your way. I'm thinkin' this has something to do with the change in your attitude lately. Now we have known for a while something ain't right, so we are gonna have a talk really soon, girl. Ya hear me?"

His eyes find mine in the rearview mirror, watching my reaction. My face must show him something because he keeps going on.

"No worries, it's not gonna happen now but when we're done at the hospital. This shit has gone on for far too long and it's affectin' you, sweetie, in so many ways. The sweet girl I've come to love over the years is struggling all alone in the dark, for some reason, while we have no idea what the fuck is goin' on or how to help ya. Daisy, we're here for you and, girl, believe me when I say you are loved. So just relax, we will make sure you get taken care of. How's the pain? Does it hurt right now?"

Nodding my head while I raise my hand, showing him a huge spread between my fingers, I lean my head back and take in all that he just said. God, Mom is so lucky to have found Des again. Especially after our deadbeat dad. He was and probably still is a jerk. Mainly because he would beat on Mom, Jagger, and me. And as much as I miss not having a dad, it's so much better all around. Feeling myself starting to drift I close my eyes for just a minute, not realizing that the drowsiness is partly because I'm extremely tired from not sleeping and partly from breathing in the mix of chemicals.

CHAPTER TWO

DAISY

Dang, how many hours have we been waiting in the ER? I think to myself. I'm so tired I can barely keep my eyes open, while my breathing is becoming more of a challenge. The smell is totally making me sick to my stomach. I'm watching the pulmonologist mix the medicine for my next dose of the breathing treatment. It's supposed to make it easier to breathe and give me some relief for the pain in my chest. From the little bit I was able to hear; when you mix bleach and ammonia together it forms a gas that can be deadly. Did not know that. Learn something new every day, as Mom always says. Anyhow, the doctor told us that when those household cleaners are mixed together, they release a toxic gas called I think he said chloramine. He said the gas can irritate your eyes, nose, throat, and lungs. It can also lead to coma and death if exposed to it for a long time. That end part freaked me out, which made me try to breathe more and I ended up choking and struggling to get air in my lungs. The nebulizing treatments are supposed to help heal the damage done to my lungs. The ER physician already told Mom I was going to need to continue the treatments at home for a couple of days. Great more crap, as usual, it just keeps piling up on my shoulders.

"Little Queen, how are you feelin'? Does it seem like the medicine is makin' it easier to breathe? Girl, you scared the shit out of your mom and me when we pulled into the emergency room parking lot. You were gaspin' for air and barely conscious. Right now, I want you to rest and do exactly as the doctors say. They say in a couple of days your breathing should get better. Your lungs are gonna take some time though, 'cause of the goddamn damage done by the gas your lungs came in contact with from breathing in that shit."

Reaching over, he gently squeezes my shoulder. Probably to get my attention as I'm drifting listening to his voice, which always calms me for some reason.

"We'll be havin' that conversation when you're up to it, okay?

Struggling to open my eyes, I look directly into his. I see the concern and love in his eyes and nod in agreement to appease him. I'm hoping we have that *talk* only when hell freezes over. Mom comes in, sees us cuddling together, and walks right up to us—arms wide—pulling us both into a family hug. I can feel her body shaking as she quietly cries. I can't help myself, knowing she is hurting not only for me but because of my actions, I feel the tears running down my cheeks.

Before either of them can say anything, the technician passes me the mask, letting me know it's time. Mom and Des give me some time alone as they leave to get in touch with Jagger and the rest of the Horde family, I'm sure. We're all family at Des's Wheels & Hogs Garage, so I am sure the phone lines will be burning up shortly.

Laying back I take deep breaths, trying to let the medicine do its job. It burns and I cough a bit, but it also helps with the pain I'm in every time I inhale and exhale. Why's this happening to me? I don't think I'm a bad person and always try to be nice and kind. What did I ever do to deserve this crap? Why does Sabrina and her mean crew hate me so much?

Thinking back, I drift off, trying to go back to when I first met Sabrina. Nothing happened between us that I can think of, so I have no idea why she despises me so much. I know she's a bully; she's always been one. She and her mean girl crew manipulate and pick on a lot of the advanced/honor students. Like me. It's like she's targeting the 'smart' kids for some reason. And I know for a fact, no one has ever done anything to her. We're definitely not the most popular kids. We are known more like some of the school's nerd population. I think that proudly as we'll never be in the popular crowd like my brother Jagger is. I've always been okay with my *nerd* standing. Well, I used to be when in middle school, but this first year of high school is really changing everything I thought I knew.

Not sure how long I've been asleep but I feel Mom gently rubbing up and down on my arms. Trying to open my eyes is a struggle, but I manage barely. As I fight to focus, the first thing I see is my mom's worried face intently watching me. Her amber eyes moving all over my face. I reach out, grasping her hand, squeezing it tightly. She grips my hand back and we sit in the emergency room, holding hands, communicating without words. Our connection has always been tight and this just makes it even more so. I can almost feel and absorb the love she is sharing with me. It encapsulates me in a safe aura momentarily. She always has had the means to make me feel safe. Even when Dad had beaten her, she made sure to let Jagger and I know, no matter what, she had our backs. I know this but for some reason still can't share what's going on with me.

The bullying at school, the eating issues I have been experiencing the last couple of months. And now the cutting. I'm praying the hospital doesn't see it, as my jeans were removed and replaced with scrubs. I cut way high on my thighs and hips, hoping that hasn't been noticed as my boy briefs are still on. My upper thighs are tingling, probably from some chemicals getting through my jeans. The pain makes me feel alive as strange as that sounds. And I have no idea why, it just does. Since the beginning of eighth grade, I started feeling emotionally removed, almost like I am emotionally dead. At first, I thought it might be my 'friend' or period. But as time went on and I got regular, the feeling didn't go away. They got worse. I haven't spoken to my queens about it though. I don't even know why I haven't shared with them. We generally tell each other everything, but this feels like it's my bullshit to carry and own. I get that it's messed up, but if I share then someone will try to fix me and take that away. Not sure I can handle my life right now without all my crutches.

At least I have some time from what Des said. They're giving me space before we have *the talk*. Just have to find a way to delay that crappy talk for as long as I can.

With Mom at my side, comforting me and holding my hand, I fall into a deep sleep without all the minutiae crowding in my head. It's been a long time since I have been able to escape in such a deep sleep.

CHAPTER THREE

CADENCE

Driving home I'm so pissed off I can feel it deep in my soul. And I don't know what to do with it. Trinity is gonna freak the fuck out, and with her being in her second trimester, I don't want to put any unnecessary pressure on her. But if I don't share what Des just told me she will flip her shit out. Damn, this not swearin' is wearing me down. At home with Hope, Trinity has beat into me that I'm not to swear in front of her. She is now two and a half, and wow, what a bundle of energy she is. Wish I had a third of that energy for Christ's sake. My ass is always draggin'.

Pulling into the drive behind Wheels & Hogs Garage, which is where our apartment is, I sit in the car for a minute. Yeah, I had to run to the store for Trinity. I'm that 'guy' now. Gettin' the grocery list from the wife and then going to the store after work. And I fuckin' love doing it. Not gonna enjoy havin' to go up and tell my girl someone intentionally hurt our Daisy. That is definitely something I don't want to do. As I'm trying to figure a way to do this, I see the door open wide. Immediately I know someone else has alerted Trinity because she has her momma bear pissed-off look on her face, which is just cute as hell. Mainly because she is anything but a badass. She looks at me, giving me the hand motions to come up.

Grabbing the bags, I manage to get up the stairs and in the house before my Lil' Hope comes running toward me, hands swinging in the air like the crazy munchkin she is.

"Daddy, Daddy, ur home. Mommy is mad at somdith with Daisssy. She has been walking back and fordt taulkin' by herself."

Dropping the bags, I pick up my little girl.

"Hope, baby, you know Daddy works downstairs every day."

"I know, Daddy, but I misd yu. Let's play, Daddy."

Putting my lil' angel down, she run-waddles down the hallway to her bedroom. Before I can even move in that direction my wife plows into me. Well, her emerging belly does, as she is showing more than with the first one. And that would be because we are having twins. Yeah, fucking twins. God friggin' help me. I can only pray that it isn't twin girls 'cause then I'm totally up shit's creek. Too much estrogen will be in our home. Gonna need all the fuckin' help I can get, and thankfully, I'm allowed to swear in my own head for Christ's sake.

"What did Des tell you about Daisy? I knew something was going on with her but with the holidays, and then the surprise wedding, my mind has been all over the place. Not to mention my pregnancy hormones. I feel so bad, baby, like I let Daisy down. Cadence, we're her family too and I should have been there for her. Remember back on Thanksgiving, she was so not herself. Her back talking to Dee Dee shocked the crap out of me. Anyway, is she okay, and who did this crap to her? Was it that little tramp who was at our wedding with Jagger? Tell me, Cadence, what you know now. Might need to get the girls together and kick some high school girls' butts. Just be prepared to get me out of jail because if we are going to do this, we are going all the way. And I'm not having our kids in the can."

Hearing her voice getting louder and more emotional, I shake my head, pulling her close, shutting her up the only way I know how. By kissing her delectable mouth. Immediately I feel the stress leave her body as she relaxes into mine. This is what it's all about at the end of the workday. Coming home to my family. After a bit, I lift my head to see her eyes at half-mast. Perfection. *I still got it*, I think to myself.

"All right, baby girl, let's get these groceries put away and I'll fill you in on what I know so far. It isn't pretty, Trinity, and I think this is just the beginning. Des did tell me that both he and Dee Dee have noticed changes in Daisy over the last nine months to a year. They thought it might be puberty and Dee Dee has even tried to talk to her daughter. Nothin' though. Daisy is zipped tight and not sharin'."

Before I can continue, I hear the cutest Mickey Mouse voice screaming...

"Daddy, cume on. The babies are waiting for you. We need to do batds and brush deir hair."

Leaving Trinity in the kitchen laughing hysterically, I head to my daughter's bedroom to play dollies. Yeah, this badass manwhore turned into a mother fuckin' pansy, participating in doll playing. And I love every Godamn minute of it. Yeah, every damn second.

After dinner, it's more playing, bath time, and bedtime stories until Hope is finally exhausted and asleep in her little big girl bed.

Trinity is on the couch, finally finding that comfortable spot with her back to the arm of the couch, stretched out kind of on her side. Both hands are on her belly, rubbing gently over the ever-growing bulge. Her pregnancy belly is much more noticeable than when she was pregnant with Hope. But God I would never breathe that to her at all. I'm not that crazy and sure don't want to die early. I slide in between her and the couch arm and start to lightly rub her stomach.

"How's my girl doin' today?"

She reaches for my hand and squeezes it, placing it on the fullest part of her tummy.

"I'm okay, feeling fuller and it seems like every day my stomach is getting so much bigger than when I was pregnant the first time. Cadence, tell me the truth, am I a fat buffalo now?"

Smiling to myself, knowin' my answer could make or break me, I look down at her, giving her one of my long hot sexy glances.

"Trinity, you're always beautiful to me. Knowing my two babies are growin' in you, damn, you have no idea what that does to me. Makes me horny as hell and I can't keep my hands off of your hot body. You get more stunning every day, baby girl."

Seeing her brilliant smile, I know I managed to miss the bullet that was aimed at my head. Thank God, couldn't take a meltdown tonight. Just want to cuddle with my girl and relax.

Shit, what's happened to me? When did I get to be an old married fuck, sittin' on the couch, rubbing my old lady's back, and actually enjoying it? Can't ever tell Des, Wolf, or Gabriel about this. They would laugh their asses off.

As we talk about our day, I realize that the guys were right, even though I will never fucking admit it. Finding the one and settlin' down is what life is truly about. I feel Trinity's body relax into mine and her breathing starting to slow down. Yep, it's another night that I'll be carrying my wife to bed. She gets tired early and usually passes out on the couch. This is one of the many gifts I've come to treasure. I take a deep breath and let her warmth take away the bullshit of my day while I pray Daisy is gonna be okay. Right now, that's all any of us can do.

CHAPTER FOUR

DAISY

When we got home late last night from the emergency room, Mom and Des never questioned me about anything. Mom settled me in and then she made me some tomato soup and a grilled cheese sandwich, both of which have always been my all-time favorites. I sat at the kitchen table while they talked about their day, like every other night in our home. No one, not even Jagger when he got home, mentioned what happened to me at school. It was like they knew I needed time to process before they threw a hundred plus questions at me. I really struggled with trying to eat some of the tomato soup and the cheese sandwich, but managed to get enough down to please Mom. When I couldn't get any more down without puking, I told her the pain was too much and couldn't eat. Not sure she believed me or not, but after dinner she helped me into my bed, after clearing a space in the pile of messy clothes scattered all over the bed. And to my utter surprise, she didn't even complain about my room being a disaster, which was a miracle in itself.

While I'm reading a book on my Kindle, a knock warns me right before Jagger walks in, closing the door behind him.

"Daisy, what the fuck happened?"

"Don't worry, Jag, everything is okay and I'll be fine too. You know how some kids are at school. Especially in high school, I'm learning. Well, you can't understand because you're one of the ultra-cool kids not like your kid sister, who falls in as one of the all-time uncool nerds. So you don't get that the rest of the population at school goes through this every day, Jagger, because of the bullies there. This too will pass I'm sure, Big Brother. Don't worry, please."

"Was it that bitch my ex, Sabrina, Daisy? Tell me because if it's her I swear to God, I'll handle this and her personally. I should have known she was trouble from the start. Wasn't thinking straight. Or as Des would say, not thinkin' with the head on my shoulders."

He wiggles his eyes at me as I make big eyes and a yucky face at him, which makes him smile my way for a brief minute, then I watch his face fill with remorse. I motion for him to sit on the edge of my bed. When he does, I grab his hand squeezing tightly. He squeezes right back then moves me gently over, so he can lie next to me, pulling me close to cuddle. It has been forever since he did this. When we were little and our dad was beating on Mom, Jagger always protected me. He even took beatings from Dad, just so he wouldn't beat on me.

I love my big brother so much. Not sure why I can't share with him about the darkness taking over my life and mind. Don't want to take the chance that if I did tell him he might not love me anymore or think I'm a crazy psycho chick. I never want to take the chance that he'd look at me differently. Even if I deserve it for reasons unknown at the moment.

"Jag, I'm exhausted and Mom gave me the medicine that is supposed to help me relax and sleep. After the next breathing treatment, I'm gonna try to get some rest. I know you're always there for me but please give me a break tonight. I need to get my head on straight first. I promise, you'll be one of the first I talk to about this once I've had some time to process. Okay, you big worrywart?"

He turns toward me, eyes probing my face. Then he pulls me to him gently again, giving me a long hug. Finally, after waiting forever for him to reply, he just nods his head while leaning down to give me a kiss on top of my head. After that he gets up, turns to leave, stopping at the doorjamb. He raises his arms to hang onto the frame. Yeah, my brother the stud muffin.

"Daisy, no matter what's going on with you, I want ya to know that I'm always here for you. And I mean that, brat. You can tell me some or all but, Sis, you need to talk about what's happenin' with ya. I know that growing up was rough for us but that's way in the past. Mom and Des are doing everything they can so we can have the best life possible. With sayin' that, I get needin' to keep shit close but this isn't the time. They intentionally hurt you, not only physically but also mentally. I can see it, Sis. So when you need me, I'm here. Love ya, little sister."

He turns and walks away before I can tell him I love him too. I can feel tears filling my eyes and when they start to run down my face they burn, but I let them continue to fall. Curling up on my bed, I hug myself as I cry tears of a very confused girl, who is feeling so alone; even though there are so many people in my corner just waiting for me to reach out and let them help me. Why can't I reach out?

I know it's a dream, but for some reason I can't wake up. My eyes feel crusty and my body recalls my dad hitting me in the head again and again, as Mom cried for him to stop. I don't even know what I did but he was furious that particular night. Mom tried numerous times to pull him off of me, but he had beaten her really badly and each time she approached, he flung her away like she weighed nothing. As the punches kept coming, I felt like I was gonna die that night. Well, that was until I heard a heart-wrenching scream and opened my swollen eyes to see Jagger pull my dad off me and throw him to the ground. Then he picked up the bat and started pummeling Dad with it. Mom and I screamed for him to stop but he was going friggin' crazy. Not sure how, but somehow my dad managed to get to his feet and started battling back with Jagger. He grabbed the bat, pushing Jagger to the floor, hitting him with the bat, then turned and just walked out the door and our lives. Forever. Never to be seen again.

Hearing Mom, Jagger, and Des, I once again fight to open my eyes. When I manage that, they are all standing around my bed, looking beyond worried. Mom sits next to me pulling me gently to her.

"My baby, oh God, baby, what's going on with you? Please, Daisy, tell me. I can't stand to see you in such pain. It's killing me, sweetie, let me help you."

Not being able to handle all this love with the darkness taking over, I pull away from Mom, moving to the other side of my bed. Mom looks crushed but Des looks at me for a minute then nods. He pulls Mom off the bed, whispering to her then they both give me a look and leave.

Jag stays in my room after they close the door. He cautiously sits on my bed, arms out. Not asking me anything, just being there for me. No expectations or demands. That's how Jagger has always rolled. No matter what, he's there to give me brotherly support.

I move into his arms as those burning tears course down my face. I'm so lost and all alone. And feeling my big brother's arm tighten around me, I don't have a clue how to make it better. This is my last thought before my mind takes over and I drift back asleep. Finally.

CHAPTER FIVE

DAISY

Mom and Des have been really cool, and extremely careful, with me the last couple of days. Mom even helped me clean and get my bedroom in order. And just saying, that was a huge undertaking. I do like everything sorted and in place, but lately I haven't had the energy to even try to clean my own room. Sitting on my bed, looking around, I feel like a guest in my own room and life. Like I'm watching time go by, minute by minute of each day, as it just passes me by. Haven't even spoke to any of my queens. Thank God Mom has been keeping them at bay, explaining to them I need peace and quiet, per the doctor's orders. Mom's being so frigging cool. Which is kind of freaking me out, because usually she just takes over and wants answers so she can try and fix crap. That's the way she has always been. In the past that was a part of her I love, but right now it scares me to death.

Also, I'm struggling because I don't get why I can't

just share my issues and explain to everyone what's really going on. Especially all the crazy crap that is running through my head. It seems like each time I try to talk to her about it a door literally slams closed in my mind's eye and the words just won't come out. I freeze and generally just walk away. Which is weird because in the past I've always been able to talk to my mom. Especially when I'm having issues and problems. She isn't like my friends' moms, who either place huge expectations on them or just don't care. My mom has always made sure I know how much she loves and trusts me. We've always had a great relationship with very few dramas. I can remember on one hand stuff I've hidden from her. She has never judged me in the past, and in my heart, I know she wouldn't judge me now. That's just not her. But again, for some crazy reason, I'm holding back even from her. What's wrong with me? Maybe those hits to the head really messed me up when I was younger and it's finally showing up now.

We've had a lot of company at the house too. Everyone from the Horde has made it a point in the last couple of days to drop by, visit, and check in on me.

Archie and Willow were first with a bag of magazines and some candy, which I won't be eating. Can't they see how fat I am? Wish I looked like them but I don't. The last thing I need is candy, my thighs and butt are big enough. But I do appreciate their kindness and it was nice to see both of them.

Then Cadence, Trinity, and baby Hope showed up. They brought me some flowers and a really cute stuffed animal Hope picked out. She was so excited to give it to me, jumping up and down, hands flying all over with the purple kitten that made even me let out a giggle. First time I've let a giggle out in a very long time, but little Hope has that effect on me and can bring such joy to my life. Even in the darkest of times. She's so innocent and truly loves me unconditionally. One of the few I feel who does. There are no limits or demands, just her looking up to me with all that love in her face. Even when I'm with Hope and I have that awesome feeling, in the back of my head is a nagging fear of when will I let her down too. There will come a day when she doesn't love me like that because I will do something to disappoint her. That's my MO, I always let folks down.

Wolf came by with a beautiful dreamcatcher he made that now hangs above my bed. He explained the story of dreamcatchers and how they are supposed to keep/catch bad dreams. He also gave me a leather pouch with some crystals and stones in it. Rose quartz to bring gentle energy to one's day, agate to ground me, amazonite to clear negativity from my mind, and amethyst for calming. As Wolf explained what each one was for, he looked into my eyes and I felt like he was reading the secret thoughts deep in my soul. It was like he was able to see exactly what I'm feeling and hiding. When he hugged me before leaving, it held so much more feeling than just two people saying goodbye. Being Native American, sometimes I get the feeling he's able to see things we don't want him to or no one else takes time to. And that really freaks me out. Especially right now in my life. I'm hiding so many things.

Then surprise of all surprises, Jag came home one day and Griffin, Cadence's little brother, was with him. Shocked as I haven't seen him except at his brother's house or the garage when there was a Horde party. Both of the guys came by my room to say "hey." Then Jagger walked down to his room but Griffin asked if he could come in for a minute. In utter shock and being totally shy because I've crushed on him since I first saw him, I just nodded. I'm such a nerd and dork. He looks kind of like Cadence, with the same build and coloring, but not as colorful as he has no tattoos. Well not yet, I guess. What he does have is some piercings on his face. His tongue, lip, and eyebrow. And he is musically inclined. He's in band at school and plays classical music as easy as he plays rock 'n' roll. All of this is going through my head, so I don't realize he's scrunched down before me until his face is right in front of me. I let out a yelp.

"Daisy, how ya doin', girl?"

"Okay, Griffin, I think. Just trying to ummm, well, get my head straight so I can go back to school. Mom and Des have been cool, but Monday is my return to school day. How are you? Finally adjusting to our school?"

Not knowing why, but he's a junior at high school when I think he should be in college or tech school. But from the little I've overheard or what I caught, he missed some school when he was younger and had to do a grade or two over. Again, so deep in my own thoughts, I don't realize I am staring directly at his face. And he's staring right back, showing nothing on that gorgeous face. His eyes are not like Cadence's, which look black but are a rich dark blue. Griff has hazel eyes with brown, green, and some gold in them. Flecks of the colors. Shaking my head, I realize he asked me something and I again have no idea what.

"What did you ask me, Griffin?"

His face splits to a small smile as he continues looking directly into my eyes.

"Lil' Flower, how're ya feeling? And you can call me Griff, if ya want."

My body tingles from his adorable nickname. No one has ever given me a nickname except Des.

"Hanging in. Like I said, been resting and giving my skin a chance to heal. The doctor says the chemical reaction is what caused the burn-redness-blisters, being I have such sensitive skin. He told Mom and me that people have done that to themselves when cleaning a tub by mixing bleach and ammonia. It's actually pretty common, I guess. You guys hanging together today?"

"Yeah, he is gonna help me with some homework that is giving me problems. Can't catch on and my teacher is a total asshole."

His eyes go to me and I swear his eyes are twinkling.

"Sorry, Lil' Flower, didn't mean to disrespect ya

with my mouth. My mom is always going on about my filthy language. I usually blame Cadence."

Not sure why but a giggle escapes my lips. He's just adorably cute and doesn't even realize it.

"Griffin Powers, I've heard worse in the hallways at our school. Not to mention the queens and I swear like truckers when not in front of the parental figures. And being a guy, I'm sure you cuss with your boys, so no need to apologize. What class is giving you problems?"

"It's advanced physics and it's pissing me off, 'cause I never have problems with any of my classes. This teacher, he's a total jerk. Doesn't explain anything and won't even come in early or stay late to help anyone in his class. All he does is assign homework from the books and that's it. Lazy jerk off, if ya ask me. Kind of lucky that Jagger is in the class. Don't know many kids in that class, so it's great that Jagger's gonna tutor me. Well, gotta say I don't go out of my way to meet new kids in my classes either. I do need this class to graduate. But enough about me and my bullshit. Heard what happened. Did you know who planned this shit and who actually did it? Jagger won't talk about it, so just wanted to get a pulse on how you're doin'. Also wanted to give you my digits so if you need me for anything, you have another person who has your back."

Having no idea why but what he said makes my heart feel so full that it hurts. My eyes fill and before I can do anything, tears are rolling down my cheeks. Griffin leans in and pulls me gently into a bear hug. And that puts me over the ledge. Sobbing in his arms when he's virtually a stranger to me is totally weird. But for some reason I feel at home and comfortable with him and in his arms. That is until I hear my big brother growl from the door. Yeah, literally growl.

"What the hell, Griffin? Let my sister go now, you fuckin' asshole. She don't need any more bullshit in her life."

Griffin slowly removes his arms, standing up, glaring at my brother for a minute. Then he turns to me, winks, and walks out of my bedroom, bumping shoulders with Jag on his way out. And just from that little touch he knocked Jagger into the wall. For some reason that brings a huge smile to my face while Jag scowls at the doorway.

CHAPTER SIX

JAGGER

What the ever-lovin' fuck? I leave this asswipe with my lil' sister for like five minutes and when I come back, he has his friggin' hands all over her. And to top it off, she is doing that ugly crying shit girls do. What the hell did he do? Stalkin' after him, I grab and pull him back, watching as he falls right on his ass. Don't even give a shit. Not at all. Wanting to kick his ass but need to check on my sister. I turn and walk back into her room and pull Daisy up and into my arms before I sit back on the edge of her bed. Lookin' up, I give the stink eye to Griffin, who's back on his feet, leaning on the doorjamb looking at me like I'm a lunatic. *Well, brother*, I think to myself, *maybe the fuck I am*. Especially when it comes to my baby sister. The time of people fuckin' with her is over.

Since all this started with Daisy, I've been rackin' my brain why she isn't talkin' to Mom or me. Especially me. It makes zero sense as we've always been close and shared everything with each other. Good or bad. No secrets. But now I don't even know what's going on with her anymore. She's withdrawn at home and seems to truly hate going to school. Each day I see her pulling farther and farther away from our family. And I mean all of us, including our extended family in the Horde.

Archie and Willow pulled me to the side, sharing Daisy didn't even get excited about all the girly magazines they brought her. This worried them both 'cause usually Daisy loves to read anything from magazines to her girly books on her Kindle. Mom said she was the same way when she was Daisy's age. Guess it's a girl thing. But I know something else is off with her. She looks sick and is super skinny. And I've noticed her color is off, even when she tries to hide it with that makeup shit she don't need. That seems to make it worse, actually. Then there is the issue of her wearing baggy clothes, including the long sleeves and pants all the time. Mom even asked me about it. She's totally freaking out about Daisy and now so am I. Des says she seems to be fightin' some demons internally, but none of us know what it is so we can't help her with it.

I've even looked up crap on my laptop, trying to find out what could be bugging a fifteen-year-old girl. The internet blames puberty and hormones a lot, but I don't really think that's it. Not to mention she has been bullied by other girls in both middle school and now it continues in high school. And if I find out who it is, well, I kinda have an idea. If it's Sabrina and her mean girl clique, I'll have something to do with makin' those bitches pay. Fuck, what's wrong with chicks? So glad I'm a dude 'cause we don't play these asinine games. And if we piss each other off, we fight it out then it's over. Not like girls. And being that Daisy is such a wonderful person, who leads with her heart and is always there to lend a hand, that's what makes everyone love her. Just don't think she's feelin' the love herself.

Feeling her bawling starting to slow down, I can feel her trying to catch her breath. I run my hand up and down her back, trying to calm her down. Feelin' his presence closer, I look to Griffin, who gives me back stink eye for a second then he leaves the room. Takin' a deep breath and letting it out, I'm just about to ask Daisy what is wrong when she beats me to it.

"Jag, all Griffin was doing was trying to calm me down. You know him better than everyone else and he would never hurt me. I don't know how I know that, but I do. Please don't be mad at him, he needs friends 'cause he doesn't have many. He was just being nice to me. And not many people are, so don't make him mad so he goes away too."

My head thrusts back as I listen to my sister. She sounds so beaten down that it is breakin' my goddamn heart. I'm gonna need to talk to Mom and Des. We need to do something immediately, 'cause I feel like I'm losing my baby sister, even while holding her frail body in my arms.

"Hey, Brat, I won't do anything to Griffin and even

if I said something he wouldn't leave. That kid is as stubborn as his big brother."

I hear her giggling, which makes me feel good so I go on.

"I was just worried to see you crying in his arms. Brat, what's goin' on? Again, I hope ya know there is nothing you can't talk to me about. Please tell me you know that?"

I feel her tense up and figure I pushed too far. She isn't gonna talk to me for some reason, but if she's comfortable with Griffin, maybe I can use the kid to find out what the hell is going on. Now that I have a half-ass plan, I gently put Daisy on her bed.

"Gonna go check on Griffin; I wasn't too nice to him. Daisy, look at me."

Waitin' for her to look up at me she takes her sweet time. I can see the apprehension all over her face.

"Lil' sis, gonna keep saying it 'til you get it. I'm always here for you, no matter what. I might not say it enough, but I love ya, Brat."

Seeing tears fill her eyes I wink her way, waiting for her cute grin, then head out to give Griff his orders.

Daisy

Watching Jag leave, I fall back on my bed, hands covering my face carefully. What the fuck is going on with me? I won't even cry in front of Mom or Des, but all but collapse on Griffin. And when he was holding me, dang it felt so good. Safe, warm, and welcoming.

Ugh, don't have time for this crap. I know that Sabrina and her girls have had their eyes on Griffin since he came to our school. He is older than Jag but because of the whole making up a class or two, they've been trying to hook up with him. Not to mention he's gorgeous. Just what he needs to not do, hook up with one of those *biotches*. I know for a while he was hanging with Heather but that didn't last. That last thought brings a huge smile to my face.

As my mind drifts, I close my eyes and instantly see Griffin's eyes. All those different colors with the gold flecks. The sincerity in them makes my heart beat faster. Damnnnn he really is cute. Then there is me sitting here looking all fat and so ugly. Immediately I have the urge to grab my secret box and head to the bathroom to make the pain go away. A couple of quick slashes would help. Thank God the weather has been cooler so me wearing jeans and long sleeves hasn't caught anyone's eyes yet. Or I pray it hasn't. Remembering the last time I cut my upper thigh, I went too deep and it bled forever. And it's taking forever to heal. Not to mention all the scars on both my legs and arms. I've even cut on my tummy below my belly button. Thinking how disgusting I am, I can't fathom why anyone as hot as Griffin Powers would waste his time on me or even want to hang together. Being so deep in my own warped thoughts, I don't hear my door open until he calls my name.

"Daisy? Ya got a minute? Want to exchange digits now, before Jagger and I get to it with this friggin' physics."

Then he smiles and once again I feel that flutter in my heart, while that voice in my head keeps telling me I'm not good enough for Griffin. Even knowing I'm wrong to do it, I move from the bed, grabbing my cell, and we share our numbers with each other. God, I'm such a silly, romantic fool. This isn't one of the books I read on my Kindle for God's sake.

CHAPTER SEVEN

DAISY

Trying to manipulate my way through the crowded hallway to get to my locker, I'm glad it's finally my lunch period. Yeah, I'm starving which is not unusual, but today I might even break down and eat, maybe some celery sticks or better yet a salad. These last couple of days at home with Mom, Des, and Jag watching everything I put in my mouth, I couldn't bring it all up. Even though it wasn't a lot of food, thinking it might have stretched my belly a bit.

Been feeling dizzy for the last hour or so, I don't want to pass out while at school. Mom would just lose herself. Not to mention, I finally will have a minute to get together with my queens to share what's been going on. Well, I'll only share a tiny smidge because they won't get off my back until I do. In each class I've heard all kinds of garbage about Sabrina and the crap her and her girls have been pulling lately with a lot of the newbies. Turning the corner to my locker, I hold in a shriek when I look up and see Griffin leaning against it, looking so frigging cute he actually takes my breath away while I stumble over my own feet. Yeah, a total nerd and klutz. What's he even doing here and how did he know where my locker was to begin with? Before I can ask these questions, he sees me then smiles that slow sexy grin of his that makes my entire body tingle.

"Hey, Lil' Flower, ready for lunch? I'm starvin', so drop your shit off and let's go."

Shocked, I stop right in front of him, knowing I must look like a dork with my mouth hanging open and confusion all over my face. Holy crap what universe am I in?

"What?"

He grips my shoulders gently, giving me a soft shove toward the lockers.

"Come on, girl, we don't have a lot of time. I'm sure your crazy-ass friends are already waitin' on you. Let's move."

He moves from in front of my locker so I can unlock and switch out my books. As I close the locker, he grabs my hand and we start moving in the direction of the cafeteria. Since school started I have never seen Griffin in my lunch period. And I would have noticed him if he was in there. Just saying, since he came into the Horde clan, I've kept a pulse on him in general. Or at least one of the girls would have. We all have agreed he is HOT.

Walking through the halls with him, I feel eyes on us and make sure mine are looking down at my feet.

That is until Griffin and pulls my hand, making me look up at him. He stops us and continues to just look at me. I start to feel uncomfortable until he pulls me closer, giving me a wink. Yeah, a friggin' wink. What's that even about? He makes me giggle when he makes a goofy face at me as we start moving back toward the cafeteria. But my head is totally up and my eyes are looking everywhere but my feet. How did he manage to do that?

I almost fall over laughing watching Akiria, Bird, V, and Amethyst's dumbfounded faces when Griffin and I make it to the table they are all sitting at eating already. My eyes wander over them and each one of their faces is funnier than the last. What? Didn't my girls think I could catch a cute guy like Griffin? Obviously, from their stupefied looks, I'm guessing they didn't.

"Lil' Flower, sit and tell me what you want to eat. I'll grab the food while you catch up with your girls."

I glance up at him from where I'm sitting, realizing I'm going to have to force some food in my mouth. And not sure I'll have time to hit a bathroom. Shit, gotta eat something or else he will wonder why I'm not eating. I've gathered he is pretty smart, in a quiet way. But dang, this is going to ruin my plans to drop another couple of pounds this week. Especially after all of Mom's food. Again, ain't got any luck.

"I'll just have a side salad."

As I reach for money from my back pocket, I hear Griffin scoff then he grabs my hand.

"No, my treat, but you have to eat something more than a salad. What are ya, a rabbit? How about a burger or slice of pizza?"

Shaking my head, trying to hide the horror on my face, I hear a throat clear behind me. It's Bird. She's the one who knows most of my secrets because she takes the time to watch and can put stuff together pretty much every time. She kinda gets why I don't want to eat. And I think she gets it because she is going through some of the same crap, which I can't understand because she is beautiful inside and out.

"Hey, Griffin, get a salad and some fries so we can split them."

She smiles at me as he shakes his head, heading over to the line for food. I watch as he is greeted by multiple people. Glad to see he is starting to make some acquaintances.

"So come on, tell us how you and him." Flipping her head at Griffin, she then looks back to me with her big green eyes."

"How, what, when, and who? Tell us all now, Daisy."

Looking at Bird, then the rest of the queens, all I give them is a scrunch of my shoulders and return Bird's big eyes. Mine are twinkling. I don't have anything to share with them as I'm just as confused. Don't even know what this is that's happening with Griffin.

Shaking my head, I look at each of them. I don't even have the words to explain current events, and more importantly, how I feel about everything.

"Okay, before he gets back, all I got is he was at our house so Jag could tutor him and he stopped in my bedroom to say hi and we ended up talking a bit. Then we exchanged phone numbers and he's texted me a couple of times, just some funny jokes, cute emojis, and crap like that. Just saying, all the texts he's sent have made me smile. What's actually happening I don't have a frigging clue, but maybe he's bored or trying to get on Jag's good side since my big brother is part of the cool, popular kids. Or more believable, he just feels sorry for me and is trying to help my brother out with his kid sister. Don't have any answers."

As they break out giggling with huge goofy smiles on their faces, I'm puzzled to why they are smiling like jackasses.

"What? It doesn't make sense to me when there are so many other girls who are drop-dead gorgeous and would probably catch his eye and do anything to keep it. I'm just an average girl so this makes me really nervous. What if he's part of the popular mean crowd, just trying to get close so they can attack from a different angle?"

Bird shakes her head furiously, her squinty eyes glaring in my direction.

"How can you say that about him? He's a perfectly damaged guy who fits you to a tee. One hundred percent. Open your eyes, sista, you both have major crap going on, and neither of you want to burden or share with anyone. That's why he is drawn to you, Daisy. Two totally messed-up souls blinded to what's right in front of each other. Can't you figure it out? Why are you always so hard on yourself? For God's sake, take a look in the mirror. You're drop-dead gorgeous with a huge heart. Take a chance, sister. I'm guessing he's totally worth it. Otherwise, your brother Jagger wouldn't be so cool with him hanging with you."

Before I can reply, I hear Amethyst clear her throat, so I turn toward her to see she's looking behind me, her eyes almost popping out of her head. Fantastic and holy crap, that must mean Griffin is probably close to our table returning with a tray of food. Stuff I don't eat and haven't for a while.

"Look who I found in line. Thought you wouldn't mind some more friendly faces."

Turning I see my jackass brother grinning huge at me.

"Hey, little brat, how's it going? Girls, hope ya don't mind me sharin' a table with ya?"

All my friends are drooling at Jag with puppy dog eyes, like I don't even know what. Bitches in heat? Like he was their lunch. YUCK! My brother, queens.

"Um well, yeah, you can join us if you want to."

I turn to look at Akiria, who's blushing and looking between Jag and Griffin. I give up because today my friends are acting like such girly losers. And yuck, Jag is my immediate family. I thought it was assumed that you don't go there...ever, I'm begging. God, see why I hate my life? Whatever. I always say it can't get worse and then surprisingly it does. *My plate is full*, I think to myself.

I shift trying to make room for Jag, but nope, not my big brother. He doesn't sit next to me, his little sister. Of course it would have to be Griff, who grabs the one right next to me. And when I look up, he is looking right back at me with a huge smile on his face like he can read my thoughts.

Crappity crap, now what?

CHAPTER EIGHT

DAISY

After lunch we all head back through the hallways to our next classes. I barely managed but was able to eat some salad, celery, and carrots. Surprisingly Griffin had a tray filled with pretty heathy stuff. Bird and V grabbed their books, taking off for their next class. Both have classes clear across campus. Jag is talking to Akiria and she's actually giving him her 'I'm interested pout.' Really? Forgetting about everything else except one of my queens and my big brother flirting with each other, I jump when a throat clears right next to me.

"Lil' Flower, where's your next class? I'll walk with you."

Shocked as no boy has ever walked me anywhere, I'm totally speechless. Especially one who looks as hot as Griff does. He kind of chuckles, probably at the look on my face.

"Cat got your tongue? Where's your next class?"

Before I can say anything, Akiria screams out loudly.

"Daisy's next class is Spanish. It's in building B. Later."

Watching her walk away, I realize it's just Griffin and me. Jagger and Akiria head off together. Oh my God, just so gross. Going to have to remind Akiria of the girl code. I grab my books, kind of slamming my locker. When I go to step around him, he lightly touches my shoulder, making me look up at him. He's watching me alertly.

"Daisy, is it okay I walk ya to class? That'll give us some time to get to know each other. Cool, right?"

I just nod. He then reaches over and grabs my book bag, swinging it on his shoulder while his hand reaches for mine. We start walking down the hallway hand in hand. Again I can feel many eyes watching us. And for once I don't care. I feel cared for, and more importantly, safe here in school, when I haven't felt like that ever since this year began.

We walk and talk for maybe three minutes then, unfortunately, I'm at my next class. He pulls me to the side and leans down to whisper in my ear as I hold my breath. He smells ohhhh so good.

"I'll be back after class to walk you to the next one. Wait for me, okay?"

"Why are you doing this, Griffin? What's going on here?"

He scratches his head, running his fingers through his hair nervously, pushing it out of his face.

"First I said use Griff. Gonna be honest here, Lil' Flower. I like you. Always have. If my head wasn't up my ass, I would have seen what was goin' on. Now that I know, it ain't gonna keep goin' on. We're at least friends, Daisy, and because of that I'm gonna make sure you're safe under my watch. That's what friends do. Now not sayin' I want you just as a friend, but you're young and I can wait. Don't get all panicky and crazy, I see it in those gorgeous amber eyes. We'll talk more later. Just know I have your back goin' forward. See ya later."

He turns, walking away, while in a complete daze I walk into my class not only in shock, but also not understanding what is happening or more importantly why. And how did today become my lucky day?

My entire day includes Griff walking me to and from my classes. To my locker to drop off or pick up books. He even waited for me outside the bathroom between classes. It feels extremely strange but in a really good way. Today is turning out to be one of my best school days so far. I haven't seen Sabrina or her mean girls all day. Well, until we were on our way to my last class. We turned the corner to see them pushing around two of the new girls, one is our girl, Mary, and the other is I think Agnes. They both seem super nice, even though I haven't gotten to know either well. Like all of us they have some issues. Just from hearing Mary talk with us, she is way concerned about her weight and about not being an honor student. She thinks she's a bit slower than everyone else. And Agnes has some acne and isn't too fashion savvy. That doesn't matter to me or my queens.

Feeling a strange vibe, I look up to see Griff's jaw tight and his eyes narrow, glaring at the girls picking on Mary and Agnes. Mary's sobbing while trying to get away from them as they pull on her clothes, hair, and make really rude and mean comments to her about her weight. Agnes is cornered against the wall by a few of them.

Releasing my hand abruptly, Griff strides right down the hall to where they all are at. When he reaches poor Mary, he gently takes her arm, pulling her away from Sabrina, putting her behind him. Sabrina looks up and instantly she licks her lips, pushing her boobs out. Really? Then for a quick minute I panic. Maybe that is what Griff really likes. And anyone can see that's the exact opposite of me. As soon as I think it, I see him give her a quick look up and down then he makes a disgusted huffing sound. Her face gets really hateful as she turns bright red when her girls start laughing. *Yay, Griff,* I think to myself.

"You better leave the girls alone, Sabrina. You don't want to piss me off. Got it?"

Sabrina looks Griffin up and down but doesn't huff. I can almost see the drool form on her lips before running down her chin. What a *biotch* on a broom.

"Come on, Griffin, we were just having some harmless fun. No harm no foul. Mary and Agnes are new so we are the welcoming crew to all the new chubbies and pizza-faces. Just like we've welcomed all the new losers when they first get here. And since both of these girls fit the definition, thought we'd kill two birds with one stone."

She laughs as Griffin turns looking back at me, then his glance goes to Mary first, then Agnes. I know what he wants without him saying a word. So I walk up to Mary, pulling her from Griff, then move to grab Agnes away from the wall. Both look at me with tears in their eyes. And so much fear, which I totally get. I wonder if that's how I've looked in the past because of their bullying.

"No worries, girls. Hey, Mary, sorry you're going through this. Didn't mean to leave you hanging, lots going on in my life right now, no excuse. Hi, Agnes, not sure you remember, my name is Daisy and that knight in the white T-shirt over there is Griffin Powers. He won't let them hurt you anymore. You girls okay?"

Agnes just stares at me for a moment as she really starts to cry, almost sobbing. Mary is trembling as she wraps her arms around herself. Then slowly she nods and opens her mouth but nothing comes out. I wait patiently as I have been right in the exact frame of mind before myself.

"Daisy, I heard what happened to you. I'm so sorry and it's good to see you doing okay. I don't know why, but they cornered both of us and started pushing me around saying stuff like, 'fatty kill yourself, such a loser, and no one wants you here so get the job done soon.' I don't even know them, have never seen them before today. Agnes and I met recently as we have a class together. We realized that we are both new so we've been texting, and just last week she told me she was at her wits' end because of these bullies. I thought if we walked together, we would appear stronger, but when they literally surrounded us and began to say such mean things, we didn't know what to do. It was like being surround by a pack of wolves. I have no idea why they are like this. Do you know why? And why pick on the two of us?"

I reach in my backpack pulling out some tissues, handing them to Agnes as I squeeze Mary's hand.

"Mary, I'm learning hateful people show up everywhere, even in high school. Don't have a clue why Sabrina is like that but she's been like that since middle school and each year she only gets worse at the bullying stuff. The problem though is she also keeps growing her mean girls, so us nerds don't stand a chance. I'm sorry you girls are going through this because it sucks. I know she picked on me before you. I've been out for a while so maybe she needed new victims, not sure. I'm thinking we need to stick together against them, no matter what. I got a group of friends or I call them my queens, so maybe y'all can start hanging with us. We've learned to never go anywhere without a buddy. Like when we were in Girl Scouts way back when."

When I finish talking to them, they both just stare at me for a moment then nod slowly and weirdly in unison. I pull first Mary then Agnes close and wait to see what Griff plans to do. It looks pretty intense, as all the mean girls are giving him hell. To his credit, he isn't backing down, throwing it right at them in return.

Suddenly a blur flies by and then Jag is shoulder to shoulder with Griff in front of Sabrina. I can tell he is so pissed by the way he is holding himself back.

"What the fuck is your problem, bitch? Didn't your parents pay enough attention to your crazy ass? Is that why you feel the need to pick on everyone? I'm sick of it, Sabrina. Knock it off now, ya get me? Don't make me have to step in."

She gives Jagger then Griffin a strange look before her face goes all crazy.

"Sure, Jagger, I'll stop...If you go back out with me. We were good together, baby, you liked everything about me, didn't you? Come on, I gave you whatever you wanted so I promise to leave them," she points in our direction with a smirk on her face, "alone if we can pick up where we left off. I miss how you made me feel, Jag. You were so nice and treated me like I was special. You remember, don't you?"

Jag steps back and before Sabrina can even put her hands on him, Griff moves in front of my brother blocking her way. He leans down and says something to her, which seems to take her breath away as her face turns white as a ghost. Then she turns and runs down the hall, not waiting for any of her bunch of *biotches*, who are following her screaming her name. *God, what did Griff say to her?* I think to myself.

Then I see him turn toward us. Both Griff and Jag head our way. Mary steps back as Agnes tenses up, but again I squeeze her hand and she looks my way hesitantly.

"Sweetie, I swear to you they would never do anything to hurt you. They're the good guys. Jagger is my older brother and Griff is his friend."

Griff and Jag come and stand in front of us. Griff checks Mary and Agnes out then puts his hand out.

"Hey, Mary, hey, Agnes, I'm Griffin Powers. What's up? Havin' another boring day, I can see."

Then he wiggles his eyebrows.

We are quiet for a second then all of us break out laughing. And for some reason we can't stop. After a couple of seconds Jag joins in. Then both guys walk all of us to our classes, which are pretty close to each other.

I'm not sure but hoping Mary and Agnes end up being the newest additions to the nerdy queen squad. Gotta talk to the girls though. We've opened our circle to others so these two more shouldn't matter. We can't let Sabrina win with all of her bullying crap. And both of them are in desperate need of some friends. Since all of us have been in the exact same spot, what better place for them to land? With all of us. And after that thought crosses my mind, I start to feel the darkness fill my mind as memories run rampant about all the times I was bullied. I try to push the feeling down but it's such a struggle. Remembering I have my special box with me, I think if I can figure out a way to get away, I might be able to let some of the pressure out. Just imagining blood running down my thigh makes me almost itch to run to the bathroom. But not with Griff and Jag with me. Can't risk it, so going to have to suck it up and find some other way to muddle through the afternoon.

CHAPTER NINE

DAISY

Waking up in a cold sweat, I'm totally disoriented at first. Then I grasp I'm safe at home in my own bed. Mom, Des, and Jag are just down the hall but my head is frigging fuzzy. Trying to lift my head I suddenly feel really nauseated. As I lie back down, I realize I didn't eat dinner tonight. Told Mom I wasn't feeling good and stayed in my room. Funny how some things seem better in my life. Like school and having Griff come into my life. Well, school is better only because of Griff.

I'm not getting bullied as much but had to watch as the mean girls turned their attention and bullying onto Mary and Agnes. And it's affecting both of them. Mary's parents have been up to school reporting it to the office, which is only making it far worse for her. And she seems to be just existing right now because the bullying is totally crushing her. Agnes also isn't handling the bullying and lately hasn't been taking care of her personal hygiene. Not being clean isn't helping her acne and her face is showing it. It is looking horrible. And her actions are starting to affect everyone around her. I like both Mary and Agnes. Truly do. They remind me of what it would be like having younger sisters, even though we are the same age. They are so naïve and immature but also funny and each has a heart of gold. Mary is always making or giving stuff to all of us girls. Agnes is so excited when we invite her to hang with us, she's that lonely thinking it's cool to hang with us. Personally, it makes me happy to try to help people who are in the same boat as me.

I reach down to rub my belly and feel my ribs poking out more than usual. Holy shit, what am I doing to myself? Why can't I just cut loose and talk to Mom? I really need to let her know I'm in deep trouble and need some serious help. Even though it makes me sick to feel the bones sticking out of my sides, it also gives me a weird and sick satisfaction that I can control something in my life. Yeah, sounds totally insane, I know this, but it's what it is. I don't even have the energy to write in my diary anymore. Even though I've got to say, I wasn't being truly honest with my writing most of the time. Why put words down in a journal or diary that are lies? So messes with the whole idea of why you're writing to begin with. I shift my legs and feel pain on my upper thigh. Also feels kind of wet. Crap, think that huge cut must be infected. I struggle to get up so I can go to the bathroom; I need to pee. No lights at first just potty—flush—wash my hands.

Bending over, I pull up the bottom of my T-shirt to see my upper thigh and gasp. The skin is a deep ruby red and has some crusty stuff around the cut, which is puffy with yucky thick yellow junk leaking out. Crap, how did this happen and why didn't I notice this? I reach for a washcloth, turning the water to warm. I go to grab hand soap but decide to get the Ivory instead. I remember Mom telling me when I was younger to wash my scrapes with Ivory because it is pure. Knowing it's going to hurt like hell, I place the washcloth on my leg. Instantly the pain is so intense it takes my breath away. Trying to take in some air I smell something bad. Is that me or my leg, don't know. Thought I showered today. As I heat up the washcloth, I notice on the far corner there is a spot that looks like a pimple ready to be popped. And being a teenage girl, I of course rub the washcloth over it, pressing down hard. It bursts and a lot of yellow pus starts running down my thigh to my knee. I almost vomit as I try to wipe it quickly. Rinsing the washcloth I swipe the area again, seeing it seems the cut has reopened. Between the pus and now some bleeding in different spots, I continue to wipe and push down on it, trying to make all the infection come out. For some sick reason my eyes are drawn to the fluids, especially the blood as it pools and runs down my thigh. The calm feeling I get from cutting takes over as I watch the blood mixed with pus and water roll down my leg. It feels like letting steam out of a pot, which then releases the pressure. I'm so intent on watching my own sick show that I don't hear the door open until I hear the pissed-off sound behind me.

"Daisy, what the fuck—I mean—what the hell is that? What'd ya do?"

Turning around I see Jag in the doorway, not even sure how I never heard him knock or open the door that has a squeak. He's so pissed off that he barges in just as I push my T-shirt back down over my thigh, trying to think how to make him get the hell out of here. I can't deal with him right now and am also so pissed and scared, so I strike out at him.

"What, don't you knock, asswipe, were you raised in a barn? I have no privacy in this house anymore. Get out now. You're my brother not my father for Christ's sake. I said get out."

Moving quickly to turn away from him, I get dizzy and, great, start to fall backward. Before I can catch myself on the sink, Jag catches me in his arms. I can feel that I'm going to puke so I turn my head as I projectile vomit all over the bathroom wall and floor. Jag gently carries me to the toilet, lifting the lid, and placing me in front of it.

"Take it easy, Brat, I got ya. Let me get something to clean that mess up before Mom or Des come in. Stay right there 'til I get back."

Watching him walk out, I feel like I'm having an out-of-body experience. Like I'm watching what is happening from above. I know from not eating all day that is why I almost passed out. Sure, the infection in my leg probably isn't helping. I'm really in deep shit. I don't even know how to pull myself out. God, why does this crap keep happening to me? Why can't I catch a break? Had a false sense of my life may be getting better. Thought with Griff around my life was on the road to getting better. But thinking on it, this might be the sign that I need help. Real help. I feel my eyes fill with tears as the weight of everything lands on my shoulders. I hear Jag come back in and all he does is grab my shoulder, giving it a squeeze. How he always recognizes what I need sometimes freaks me out. Then he proceeds to clean my puke off the wall and floor. All I can comprehend at this moment is damn, I have the best friggin' brother out there.

Sitting on the bed in Jag's room, I know this is going to be extremely difficult. Not sure how or if I can open up to anyone, even my awesome big brother. He walks in with a glass in his hand and some crackers.

"Drink this ginger ale and eat these crackers. Mom would give this to us when our stomachs were upset."

I take the glass but not the crackers. He literally glares at me.

"Jag, I'm watching my weight. You know that because I've told you many times. I have to watch my carb intake. And do you know the amount of carbs there are in crackers?

"Really, Daisy? That's the best you got, Sis? You're skin and bones. You haven't noticed Mom makin' every one of your goddamn favorite meals the last couple of days, just to get you to eat. And if you think I don't know what you are doing, you're nuts. I see you barely eat then immediately go to the bathroom. What do you think, I'm stupid? I know what you girls do to lose weight. All that stupid shit, for what? Why do you care what other people think? You didn't need to lose weight in the first place. What's really bothering you anyway?"

Staring at my big brother—who I have idolized forever—seeing the anger and hurt in his eyes breaks me.

"I had to lose weight, Jag, maybe then they would leave me alone. And it did work, somewhat. They're still jerks, bullying and intimidating me but nothing like before. Not sure if it's all the weight I lost, Griff always being around, or because they have moved on to Mary then Agnes. I just don't want them to come back to me. You don't understand how cruel they are. Even without the constant bruises, my arms still always hurt. The pushing and knocking me down, flinging me into lockers 'accidentally' and all the crap. And not having them post crap on my Facebook page is such a relief. To be able to walk into a bathroom at school and being able to go pee and not pee in your own pants because they won't let you in a stall. No, you won't ever get it."

At this point snot is running out of my nose as tears are flowing down my face. I'm totally losing it. But he still doesn't know it all.

"Jag, you don't get it because you're one of the cool dudes. You hang with the cool crowd. No one calls you names, makes fun out of how you look—what you like—or who you hang with. They don't push you around, pinch, punch, or grab you so hard it leaves bruises. They don't pull your hair so hard that it feels like they are pulling it from your scalp. They don't constantly rag on you until you start to believe what they are saying. I think sometimes that I'm losing my mind. It's not like Mom says, those teenager hormones. I wish it was. I can't sleep, eat, go to the bathroom, yeah, I know TMI. I'm cold all the time and have caused myself injury on purpose, just to feel something—anything. I don't remember the last time I told you, Mom, or Des that I love you. That's because I don't even know what those words mean anymore. I feel nothing but darkness in my life."

Taking a deep breath, I reach over grabbing the tissues he is holding out. I wipe my face and blow my nose. Looking into his eyes I feel it, and for once—thank God—can't stop the words from bursting from my lips.

"Jag, I'm hurting real bad. My troubles are huge and I don't know what to do. I'm falling and not sure if I can or even want to get up anymore. I've had really bad thoughts too. Probably just like every other kid who's being or been bullied."

Looking at my brother as tears drip from his face, he reaches over and pulls me into his lap, rocking me as he gently holds me to his chest. For the first time since I can't remember, I actually feel something. Safe in his arms and his love. And before I fall asleep I barely hear the words he whispers to me.

"Daisy, Brat, I got you. And know this, love you, little sister. Love you. You're safe now. That's my promise to ya."

CHAPTER TEN

JAGGER

Lookin' at my kid sister sleeping restlessly in my bed, the fuckin' emotions I'm feelin' are so goddamn overwhelming. *I let her down* is the first thought that runs through my brain. Holy shit, I'm angry as a motherfucking rabid dog. What the hell happened to Daisy for her to want to hurt herself? As my eyes take her in, my mind registers that cutting isn't the only way she's hurting herself. Actually, taking her in, she is skin and bones. Dieting my ass—not eating—starving herself because some crazy-ass loser bitches are telling her she's fat, which is such a goddamn lie. As my heart feels like it's tearing right down the middle, I think to myself, *my God what did that bitch Sabrina do?* I know deep in my soul that she has had a hand in beatin' Daisy down. What did I ever see in her? After a quick thought I know what I saw in Sabrina. Being a horny teenage asshole guy with a chick that was as easy as her, who gave it away, with no work on my part. And once I had a taste, nothin' was going to keep me from gettin' me some. Yeah, I was like a raging male fuckin' dog chasing after a bitch in heat. That's what she turned me into and all that was on my brain. Thinkin' only with my dick and gettin' off was it. No idea at all that the chick I was fuckin' around with was brutalizing my sister. I didn't know it, but unintentionally gave her direct access to Daisy. In the only place she should have felt safe—in our home. I sit on the side of my bed, puttin' my head in my hands, trying to figure out what to do next. It stops now for my little sister.

Hearing Daisy rolling, flipping, and moaning in pain, I move off the bed and actually look at her for a moment. Damn, she looks seriously ill. Daisy's awfully pale, her coloring way off, almost grayish, while it seems like she is strugglin' to breathe. Immediately I stand, gently grabbing Daisy's shoulders as I shift her in my bed, moving her to one side. She instantly lets out a sigh, which seems to let her breathing start to regulate. I put her down, go to her room, and get her inhaler in case she was gonna need it during the night.

Fuck, as pissed as Daisy is gonna be at me I need to talk to both Mom and Des immediately. She needs help and I don't think we can give her what she needs. Remembering back to the beginning of the school year, I realize how worried I was about Daisy startin' high school. My lil' sister looks just like our mom, who is drop-dead gorgeous. All my buds always talk about Mom like she isn't my mom but a MILF, and it grosses the fuck out of me. So knowin' this I couldn't help but worry that boys of all ages would be chasing Daisy. Instead, my mind and body got caught up with Sabrina when she took over my life, leadin' me around by my dick. My concern for Daisy left my mind the minute Sabrina manipulated me and got down on her knees. Damn, that bitch was wild but I knew deep down she was also bat-ass crazy. Some of the shit Sabrina ranted about started to freak me out. Then I had heard from a couple of my buds that I wasn't the only one she was spending *time* with. Then after catching her with Daisy one too many times and my lil' sister on the floor, it slammed into me that every single time Sabrina was in our house Daisy was either fallin' or gettin' up rubbing her arms slowly. I started to put shit together. Then at Cadence and Trinity's wedding, the shit Sabrina pulled was the last straw. She had the nerve to throw it in my face that I took everything she offered. Really? Fuck, what guy wouldn't take what was being thrown in your face? Well, one guy comes to mind: Griffin, Cadence's younger brother. I realize I wasn't thinkin' straight. Des always warned me while growing up about not thinking with the head on my shoulders. God, he was so right, why didn't I listen?

Lettin' out a soft laugh before it hits me, I let Daisy down by not bein' there for her or setting a better example. Especially with having Sabrina here when Mom and Des weren't home. I disrespected my entire family. And that bitch was loud, so guessin' my little sister knew exactly what was goin' on in my bedroom. I'm such an asshole.

As my fingers comb through my hair, I go to my closet, pulling out my sleeping bag. A night on the floor is nothin' compared to the hell I envision Daisy has been going through. Fuck!!! When did I forget about her? How did I not see the warning signs I'm sure were right in front of my face for Christ's sake? We've always watched out for each other since Mom left our asshole father. No, I call him the sperm donor, he doesn't deserve the title of 'father or dad.' He was a constant jerk, always beating on Mom first then me as I got older. Mom always tried to get him to stop and he would stop hitting me and then rain down hell on her. I know he did hit Daisy a couple of times when Mom wasn't home, and he threatened both of us that if we told, neither of us would remain breathing. Finally, Mom caught on when she saw a bruise on Daisy's arm and she made the move to leave him. Then that last time, when I beat the shit out of him, Mom didn't wait any longer. Thank God we both were home or I think he would have killed Daisy. And even though it was totally hard to start over with two young kids, our mom did it and she changed our lives forever. Well, that was until Des came into our lives. But somehow we all got lost in our daily lives and left Daisy behind.

As I spread the sleeping bag out, I think back on our childhood. As kids we were always together. Mom started workin' for Des after she left our sperm donor and I know the Horde did something to make sure he didn't show his face again. And he never has in all these years. But they also saw the damage he did to our mom and us kids. That last fight was very violent. I ended up with a black eye and fat lip for getting between Mom and him. Daisy's wrist was sprained and she had goose eggs all over her head and bruises on her face and shoulders. Not to mention the damage that was done to Mom. She was covered in bruises and I think she had a couple of bruised or broken ribs. Des stepped up and took care of everything. Even back then I looked up to him. He's a total badass, no doubt, but he takes care of our mom 'cause he cares for her and doesn't give a flying fuck what anyone thinks. He helped her find a safe place to live and all the guys from the Horde would step up whenever we needed something. Those first couple of years were rough, especially for Mom. Des even gave her a job as the manager of his Wheels & Hogs Garage. And though Des knew she could do the job, Mom felt she had to prove to all that she was worthy. Her confidence had been badly beaten from her. But as time went on, I could see there was something between Mom and Des. Thank God we've never heard from our dumbass sperm donor again. With time we all managed to heal with Des's and the Horde's help.

Lyin' down, I wonder if that damaged part of our life somehow made Daisy more accepting to believe and take Sabrina and her friends shit and all the bullying they did to her. Because that is what they were doing. It's a known fact throughout school to stay away from her and her bitch-ass girls. I never thought she would go after Daisy. But maybe in my kid sister's mind she figured she deserved it for some reason. We avoided talkin' about the physical or verbal abuse we suffered at the hands of an asshole. It kind of got shoved into the closet and left there. We just buried it and now maybe I think we should have gone to some kind of counseling or something.

Yawnin' I realize how goddamn tired I am, when I close my eyes seeking sleep. Right before I doze off, I hear a sniffle telling me Daisy is up. Not saying anything, waiting to see if she will reach out, I lie on the floor waiting. Hearin' the springs in the bed squeak as she sits up, I impatiently wait for her to call out to me. Want her to know that I'm here but the first step has gotta come from her—she needs to actually ask for help. Right when I'm thinkin' she's gonna flee to her room, I catch a soft and garbled sound from her that breaks my heart.

"Jag, are you awake? Jagger, please, I'm scared."

I jump up and sit next to her, pullin' her into my arms while my mind is unable to comprehend how thin she feels. Her body starts to tremble. I feel her body tense and know she is tryin' not to cry.

"Daisy, let that shit out. Listen to me, Brat. No matter what's goin' on we can get through it as long as we do it together. Remember how Mom always used to say nothing can hurt us unless we let it. Come on, Daisy, we went through all kinds of hell and we can't let anyone or anything beat us back down. You're so much stronger than you think. Let it out. Tomorrow we'll talk with Mom and Des and figure this shit out.

Together as a family. But tonight it's just us. Damn, I forgot what Mom used to call us. Her very own ying and yang."

I hear her giggling softly and I'm hopin' to Christ I didn't make this worse. In the morning we are gonna have a family conversation. And just sayin' I, for one, am gonna take down names and kick some major ass.

CHAPTER ELEVEN

DAISY

Feeling like my head is filled with bricks, my eyes seem glued shut. I try to pull myself from the deep sleep I'm in. Slowly as my crusty swollen eyes open, I realize I'm not in my room or own bed but Jag's. Trying to shake the utter confusion from my brain, I sit up on the edge of his bed. Looking around I see his sleeping bag on the floor, but he's not in it. Not sure what time it is but am thankful it's Saturday. That means no school so I can rest my head in my outstretched hands. I start to rock back and forth trying to calm myself. Realizing my secret is out and that Jag figured out what has been going on; he won't be quiet about it. He's a git 'er done type of guy. I vaguely remember him telling me something about talking this out with Mom and Des. Remembering that statement makes the anxiety in me reach new levels. As my panic hits, I have absolutely no clue what to do. There's a part of me that wants to finally confide with my family. Truly I do, but the other part is scared to death that they are going to put me in a hospital or wacky ward. Mary shared she was in one over last summer and I think one of the queens also was in one, but no one ever talks about it. I'm not the only secretive one apparently. Mary is struggling right now and Agnes shared that her parents are making her visit a shrink to see why she is so depressed all the time. We all know why. The mean bitches haven't been bullying me as much because they have been concentrating on Mary and Agnes. On one hand I feel really terrible, but on the other hand, I'm so relieved because that means the crazy witches on brooms aren't paying as much attention to me. And that thought tears me apart. Hearing the door creak open, I turn to see Jag walking in with a steaming cup in his hand.

"Hey, Brat, brought you some of that shitty hot tea you like. How're you feelin' this morning? Did you sleep good?"

Hearing his voice I can tell he is nervous.

"Jag, doing okay, I guess. Just really confused and scared to death. Thank you for being there for me last night. Sorry I had a major meltdown. School and all that other crap is totally getting to me."

"Daisy, we know it's more than school. I already told both Mom and Des we need to talk. Before you go all crazy on me, I didn't say why. They're both at the shop 'til noon so you have until then to figure out how ya want this to go down. One thing though, either you'll tell them or I will, but this eating thing is something we need to put on the table. And the other shit you been putting up with and doing is also gonna be brought up. I know you are gonna be pissed but I was up early and looked through your room. Don't give me stink eye, lil' sis. You've been hidin' shit from me and it has been goin' on long enough. Damn it, Daisy, when did you start cuttin'?"

Dropping my head back down, I feel my anxiety crawling up my back to the front in my stomach, then all the way up to my throat. I feel like vomiting but don't have anything in my belly to bring up. They will all find out now and look at me like I am crazy. Nothing I can say or do will stop them from realizing how weak I truly am. I'm not like any of them. Mom, Des, and Jag are so strong and can do or handle anything. I'm weak and have nothing to offer anyone. That feeling keeps growing inside of me until my head is filled with all the usual negativity. I knew this day would come eventually, just didn't think it would be this soon. Getting up I brush past Jag without a word and head to my bedroom. Need to figure out how I can begin to explain what's been going on with me recently. I don't want to lose the only people who believe in me. I'm so screwed. More than that, I'm scared to frigging death and totally fucked.

The waiting is literally killing me. Knowing I'm going to have to face my family soon makes the tea I've been drinking feel like it's ready to shoot out of my mouth onto the floor. I'm sitting in my bedroom just sitting and waiting. My queens have been texting like crazy and once again I'm just ignoring them. I can't face them too and try to explain how I feel or what's been going on right now. They won't get it because their home lives are very different. Not perfect but still way different than mine. When I tried one time to explain everything, I forgot who had asked me if I had PTSD from growing up with an abusive dad. One who liked to beat on my mom and us kids when he could. I never answered that question because I didn't know the answer.

Hearing the car door slam outside my time for reflection is almost over. My mind is petrified that my secure place in this household with my family will come to an abrupt end after this talk. Once I bare my heart and soul to everyone, they will see me for the weak baby I truly am. Unable to deal with life in general. Then they will either try to change me, force me into more counseling, or they will start to fade. Like everyone does. Being weak is not something people hope to achieve in their lives. Murmuring is coming from beyond my door as I sit patiently on my bed, rocking back and forth. My anxiety is at an all-time high and I don't want to do this. Not ever. Letting my family see the *real me* is terrifying. Not only that but to tell them about the bullying crap I've been putting up with from Sabrina. Especially Jag, since he was dating her and knew her 'biblically.' That thought alone makes me giggle. Yeah, he knew her as they say biblically. And unfortunately, I heard that crap firsthand. Yuck, that thought turns my belly even more.

With everything going through my mind, I try to enjoy the quiet in my bedroom and mind, closing my eyes. Just for a minute or two. Or so I think.

My eyes attempt to open when I feel someone gently shaking me. When I can focus I see my mom sitting beside me, concern written all over her face.

"Daisy, my baby girl, how are you doing? I let you sleep for a couple of hours. Don't want you to sleep the entire day away though that's why I wanted to wake you."

Hearing her makes me look down. I am covered with a throw from our couch and realize that I must have fallen into a deep sleep. Guess my body knows what I need more than my mind does.

"Honey, I brought you some hot tea, do you want to drink it in here or come out to the kitchen? I cut up some fruit and cheese for you to snack on until dinner."

Giving me an opportunity to say no, I almost take it until I see my mom's face. The pain in her face breaks my heart. I did this to her. After all she has done for me my entire life, I'm hurting her with all this bullshit. What makes it worse is she's always been there for me. Crappity crap, I need to put my big girl panties on and face the music.

"Yeah, Mom that sounds good. I could eat. A little something, I guess. Let me grab my phone."

Instantly her face brightens and one of her dazzling smiles is directed at me. Just seeing that warms my heart. How do I keep forgetting how lucky I am to have this woman as my mom? What a role model. All she has ever done over the years was do what she could so Jag and I would have a good life. How did I forget that? All the stuff she does to make sure we are safe, have not only a house but a loving home and food. Not to mention the daily struggles she personally endures. I'm such a dummy.

Following her into our kitchen, I plop into a chair as she brings the steaming mug filled with my hot tea. On the table is a platter with all kinds of cheese and fruit, so I tentatively reach for a square of cheese and try to start munching on it. After a couple of times, I manage to swallow, and I realize this is the first time in a long time I've eaten something willingly. Without worrying about counting calories or being fat or whatever sick things that have been going through my head.

"Daisy, you know we have to talk. I've asked Des and Jagger to give me some time alone with you, hoping this would make you more comfortable. You know there isn't anything you can tell me that would shock me, or more importantly, make me love you any less. You know that, sweetie, right?"

Hearing those words shakes me to my core. Again, I think how the hell I could forget what a phenomenal woman my mom is? God, am I losing my mind? Why did I forget how lucky I am with the family I was blessed with? How could I? Truly don't want to upset her but what would she think of me if I told her I ate an entire pie, puked it up in a mixing bowl, and sat there just looking at it forever before flushing it down the toilet? Yeah, not going to be putting that kooky shit out there. Probably would give them the perfect reason to lock my psycho butt up. Well, guessing it's time to try and act my age.

"Mom, I know that but thanks for reinforcing it. I'm just going through some really deep stuff like, you know, 'teenage crap.' My head is always confused with all kinds of dark thoughts all the time. I want to try and make the most of all the opportunities available to me. Not to mention all the things I want to see and do. But I keep making bad choices and can't even explain it. I feel like demons are in my head and every so often they just take over. I can tell when because people ask stupid questions like 'are you okay' or 'what's up?' When this happens, I usually ignore all those questions. I don't even know what any of you want from me but I don't have anything else to share. That is except I know you guys plan on trying to get in my head to figure everything out and fix it. But, Mom, you can't fix everything in my life. I'm messing up but what if this is happening because I have some disease or illness? I feel like my elevator isn't stopping on all of my floors. Hell, I don't even know what that even means. Do I have some issues? Yeah, but so do many kids my age. We're trying to figure everything out while growing up, going to school, figuring out our path in life. What happens after school? What do I do? Do I go to college or get a job? Go into the military maybe? I'm just trying to cope with all those questions that are going full circle in my head all the time. Not to mention trying to fit in. I won't ever be considered a popular kid, Mom. I'm so very sick of trying, it just doesn't work. My friends, or as we call each other queens, are slowly pulling away. Not sure if it's my fault or theirs, I can't figure it out. I feel so isolated, Mom, but don't have any idea how to fix it. I've done things I'm not proud of but don't know how to stop. It's escalating daily and getting dangerous. I'm drowning with no rope or life jacket. I'm feeling all alone. Probably just like Mary and Agnes are feeling every day. And I'm scared to death that you guys are gonna lock me up in a loony ward."

Putting my head down, I feel the tears running down my cheeks. Not hearing anything but my stupid phone vibrating constantly, telling me I have text after text coming in. So worried about who or what the texts say I'm shocked when a finger lifts my head so gently. Then I am looking into Des's eyes. So deep and penetrating. He pulls me up and into his arms as his hands run up and down my back. I can feel the love he has for me. Especially when Mom comes next to him, reaching over and squeezing my shoulders. Why can't I trust this? Or for that matter, when did I stop trusting Mom and Des? They are totally the shit, as Jag always says. Not sure what the hell is going on but I'm starting to realize my big brother is right—I need to trust my family. No one says anything but Des keeps rocking me in his arms. Mom's hands gently go up and down my back in a comforting manner.

For the second time in forever I feel protected. I am circled in their love for me. And I can actually feel it.

CHAPTER TWELVE

DES

Holdin' Daisy I know the road ahead is gonna be filled with a ton of ups and downs, for sure. Goddamn it for fuck's sake, this child in my arms is suffering and it's up to Dee Dee and me to get her back from whatever demons are chasing her. Hearing the back screen door slam, I look up to see Jagger staring at me. He raises his eyebrows at me, and for a moment, I think to myself, *Shit, when did that little boy from way back become such a grown man?* Fuck he's only a senior in high school but he's the one who demanded this family meeting as soon as he realized Daisy was in trouble. I'm so proud of him.

Gently I lean Daisy away from me.

"Hey, Little Queen, get yourself together, we need to do this, okay?"

Watchin' her nod, she moves away from me, taking a seat in her chair, grabbing her hot tea taking a sip, eyes down. I look from Dee Dee to Jagger and we all nod then take our seats. Daisy's phone is constantly jumping all over the table vibrating. She keeps looking at it almost as if she is scared to see who it is texting her. Another thing to add to the list of shit to figure out. What the fuck is goin' on? What young teenage girl doesn't grab her phone every time it buzzes for Christ's sake?

The four of us look from one to the other for a couple of minutes before I turn to Jagger, giving him a slight nod.

"Daisy, I told you earlier that I had spoken to both Mom and Des. Today we're just gonna have a conversation and see where or what to do next. Before we start, I need to share some things I've discovered."

"Jag, don't you dare, that's not yours to share!"

As Daisy and Jagger shoot daggers at each other, I clear my throat.

"All right, you two, calm the fuck down. Remember when we're at this table any subject is open for discussion, and no matter what, we leave all our negative feelings here. We don't let shit come between our family. No matter how much it hurts. We've had some pretty intense talks right here and very few rules apply here. That's how our family works, and we've made this deal a long time ago. So sayin' that, Jagger, continue carefully."

I feel Dee Dee grab my hand under the table and I give it a squeeze. Glancing her way, I see every worry, concern, and emotion on her face. She could never hide her feelings. Givin' her a squeeze, I place her hand on my upper thigh and give my full attention to Jagger.

"So while Daisy was sleepin' I went through her room, lookin' for some clues as to what's going on with her. I get the shit at school with being a freshman. But this is so much more. First, I found a journal/diary, or whatever chicks call them, in which she has recorded everything. From what she has eaten, exercise she has done, and the purging she has done when her weight hasn't gone down. I'm guessin' Daisy has—well damn—hate to say it, but maybe she has an eating disorder."

As Jagger finishes I hear Dee Dee gasp. Glancing her way, she is pissed.

"Jagger, you should have never gone through your sister's bedroom and personal items. I can't believe you did that, Son. We don't violate each other's trust in this house."

"Mom, what do you want to wait for? Until she passes out—falls down the stairs—hits her head goes in a coma; or her heart gives out from the stress and lack of nutrition. Look at her, Mom. I mean, Mom, really look at her. Daisy is a bag of fuckin' bones."

Vaguely listenin' to the banter between Jagger and his mother, I watch Daisy's face. There's no emotion at all. It's almost like she isn't even here, well at least not in spirit. Her body is takin' up space but that's it. I feel fear go up my spine as I continue to watch her as both Jagger and Dee Dee get into it loudly. Nothin'. She's watching them as if you would watch a television show. Reaching down, I grab Dee Dee's hand, squeezin' it to get her attention. As she glances up at me, I give a head nod toward Daisy so she turns and looks at her daughter. We both do and eventually Jagger catches on and shuts up when he realizes what we're doin'. All three of us are staring directly at her, and absolutely nothin'. No emotions or reactions from her at all. I can't take it anymore. It's killin' me to see her like that.

"Daisy girl, look at me. Come on, beautiful, give me those gorgeous eyes."

Not sure what actually penetrated but she finally looks like she is waking up from a nap. She shakes her head like she is clearing the fog, and I actually can see when it hits her that we were all staring at her. Her face shows shock that we saw how much she was mentally removed from us. She looks at me with wet, scared eyes.

"Have ya been listening to your mom and brother at all? Daisy, they were havin' words about you—where did you go? Can ya tell us?"

Looking at me with the saddest expression on her face, she lowers her head. I barely make out her response as she whispers it quietly.

"Des, I don't know, I just get in my head. I honestly don't have a clue what they were saying, even though I was watching their mouths move. I'm sorry. So sorry. This has been happening more and more. I lose time. Sometimes it happens in school or in a class. It's happened here at home too. I tend to lose large amounts of time now and then, and I don't know why. I'm drawing up a blank or when I feel totally alone and have dark moments is when I don't remember at all."

Before I can get a word in, Jagger bein' the angry teenage asinine boy he can be sometimes goes all-in screaming directly at her.

"What the hell, Daisy, how can ya not know what we were saying; you're sittin' right there, damn it? Is this your way to get around the anorexia, bullying, and cutting conversation? Because I'm not dropping it, Brat. Mom and Des need to know how serious this shit going on is. Show them your arms, Daisy. Ya know what I mean. Upper arms, underneath. Let them see the cuts and scars of what you've been doin' to yourself. Not to mention the infected cuts on your upper thighs. Also, why the fuck haven't you told me about the shit at school? You know I always have your back, Sis. Since we were kids, durin' some of the worst times in our lives 'til one of us dies, I'll always be here for you. I love you, lil' Brat."

Dee Dee pulls away from me, stands up and goes to her daughter, pulling Daisy into her arms. Then she turns and her troubled amber eyes are shooting flames at her son.

"Jagger, ENOUGH. Attacking Daisy with all of these things at once isn't helping, Son. We are supposed to be here to show her she is loved and we support her. You're beating her up with your accusations. It's not making this horrible situation better."

As soon as Dee Dee is done addressing Jagger, Daisy pulls away from her mother. As I watch her, she starts to hyperventilate, her arms going around herself. She is rocking back and forth looking from Dee Dee to Jagger and back again. Finally in a loud shriek, Daisy starts yelling and swearing.

"Mom, don't get mad at Jag. All my life he's had my back, even when we were little and Dad used to beat the crap out of us. How many times had he taken beatings and crap on my behalf? Let's face it, right now, I'm not strong like you guys. I'll say it right now out loud that I'm the family loser. Today proves it, with all that has been said. And it's all true. I'm constantly watching my weight and how much I eat. I'm counting carbs and I can't eat without making myself puke. Now I'm cutting myself just to be able to feel. Feel anything —something—anything—even if it's just my own pain. Between the bullying, not eating, and cutting, I don't even know who I am anymore. I've lost me, Mom. Sometimes I wish that I would fall asleep and never wake up. So is that what you want to hear, Mom? Because that's how I truly feel. I can't be perfect like you are. Never could. And at this point I don't even care anymore. Just can't because I'm so tired."

When she finishes, Daisy is gasping for air, rocking back and forth, her eyes all moving over the place anxiously. Her face is covered with a light sheen as her entire body is trembling. Before I can even reach her and Dee Dee, she pulls away again. A torturous scream comes from deep down. Shocked I just stare, never heard Daisy do anything like this before. "Everyone, just leave me alone. I can't take all of you staring at me with eyes filled with your damn pity. Let me be for God's sake. Maybe it would be better for all of you if I wasn't alive. Death is looking better and better. Then no one would have to worry or pity me. You could just live without poor little Daisy totally messing things up. I can kinda get why people try to or even do kill themselves. To stop the torture. I'm tired and want some peace."

I watch as she gets up and turns, running to her room. She collides with Wolf. He pulls her close to him, holding tightly as he watches her like a hawk. She's frozen in place so he leans down whispering in her ear. I see exactly when Daisy lets go 'cause Wolf lifts and carries her to her room, givin' me a look I've seen before.

Tryin' to keep the two people who care for Daisy more than anyone in the kitchen is a fuckin' nightmare, not to mention a goddamn battle. Dee Dee is bad enough, but Jagger is a boy, who is more grown man with tons of strength and determination to get to his kid sister. His protector mode is at full peak. Before I have to resort to actually putting hands on him, Wolf appears back, his face is troubled.

"Daisy is in lying down. Not gonna try to tell you what to do but whatever just happened wasn't workin'. Y'all are way too close. She's in a very bad way. Needs professional help immediately. Has she seen that counselor Trinity recommended?"

He looks at us as we shake our heads. Dee Dee moves to Wolf, wrapping her arms around his waist.

"Wolf, her appointment is set for Monday. Oh my God, she is so much worse than I could have imagined. How did I not see all of this and her struggles? I've failed her. So much that she's hurting herself physically just so she can feel something, whatever the hell that even means. She's my daughter for Christ's sake, how did I not see this?"

"Dee Dee, teenagers are good at hiding. Especially ones who are in trouble, be it physically or emotionally. That is why no one has recognized the signs. Not to mention she's a girl with her emotions and hormones all over. Don't be too hard on yourself, 'cause she's gonna need all three of you in her corner. She's got a long road ahead of her."

We all take a seat around the kitchen table as Jagger fills in Wolf with all he's discovered about Daisy. I watch my friend close his eyes, trying to absorb all that he's being told. Out of everyone in the Horde, Wolf prides himself as the 'family protector.' Even to his own detriment. Seeing him react, I know we're all gonna take responsibility and even blame. We feel like we let down our child and it happened right before our eyes. Wolf's shoulders fall forward as he runs his hands down his long black hair, head hanging low. The weight on his shoulders has become much heavier now as he comes to terms with how bad it is. Wolf, as long as

I've known him, has been the caretaker of the bullied, injured, and abused. Both in humans and animals. We all just found out recently about his work with those who have survived life's atrocities. He even went as far as to start a safe haven at his ranch for those in need. We're gonna need to pull from his resources 'cause he has more experience with this shit than any of us.

After Wolf leaves, Jagger goes off to his room. Dee Dee looks in on Daisy, seeing she's out like a light. After locking everything down, I join Dee Dee. We lie next to each other in our bed, holding each other for dear life. Tryin' to pull her closer, knowin' how she's suffering from all the shit now that we are up-to-date. And from what Wolf explained to us, it's gonna be a long bumpy road 'til it starts getting better. Fuck, as usual, just how life works unfortunately. Gotta get to the root of the problem though. I have no words that can fix this. All I know is we have a long hard road ahead of all of us to bring Daisy back.

"Sugar, no matter what, we'll help Daisy through this. As long as we work together there isn't anything we can't do."

Hearin' her sniffle, I pull her closer as she snuggles against my body. Tonight, no words will help but I have other ways of makin' my Dee Dee feel better. Reaching down I use my forefinger to lift her head, as I gaze into those amber eyes I fell in love with all the way back in high school. Shifting down, I gently kiss her full lips. Tonight, I will take her mind off of all this bullshit by makin' my woman feel good. Tomorrow we start taking the steps to try helping our girl heal. Life as we all know it will definitely change.

CHAPTER THIRTEEN

GRIFFIN

Not bein' able to reach Daisy all day has me fuckin' worried. I know shit's goin' down and want to be there for her. Well, at least as her friend, even though I wish for more someday. Damn, I'm such a damn idiot, should have been payin' attention.

As I continue my daily jog through the park, I think back to the last couple of days. I've finally got to spend time with Daisy at school, walking with her to and from all her classes and eatin' lunch. She and her crazy as shit girls are totally nutty. When she isn't in her head Daisy's a riot. Yeah, she's shy, quiet, and reserved but I kind of dig that for a change. Especially since I'm not a huge talker myself and would rather just be. I'd rather have a girl like Daisy than the sluts who are always throwin' themselves at me. Well, gotta say I've changed my ways since that one time Daisy saw me with Heather. Just seeing the hurt on her face gutted me. Always had my eyes on little Daisy, but was fillin' time 'til she got a bit older. Also 'cause my brother Cadence said he'd kick my ass if I didn't wait. Funny coming from the biggest manwhore around.

Driving from the park home while drinking a Gatorade, I feel my phone vibrate, so at the next red light I reach into my pocket, grabbin' it out, looking at the display. Not recognizing the number, I almost don't answer. But for some reason I feel my gut tighten and it's like someone is telling me to pick it up. Weird as shit feelin'.

"Yo it's Griffin."

"Dude, have you been on Facebook today? What a fuckin' huge shitshow. That bitch, Sabrina, and her mean girl hos have been goin' nonstop at that new fat chick ya know, think her name is Mary. Can't believe the shit they're spewin' all over social media. This is worse than all the other shit they've put out there."

"What? Dillon, are you serious? What a bunch of fools, why are they posting it out there? That shows how stupid they are. And, asshole, don't call any chick fat, you dick. No wonder you can't get a girl to go out with ya ugly ass."

Listening to my friend blunder through his explanation I make it home. Rushing through the front door, I immediately head to my room, powering up my laptop, and signing into my Facebook account. What the fuck? I can't believe my eyes as I see Sabrina's page and all the bullshit she's posting. Son of a bitch, anyone would crumble under this type of bullying and pressure. And just thinkin' the little I know about

Mary, she doesn't seem like she's emotionally strong. Not to mention she's new and doesn't have her own friends or a group of girls who have her back. She's been on the verge of a major breakdown since I first met her that day I stepped in. Daisy and I have tried to keep her spirits up, but damn it, can only do so much. When you're called loser and other shit for so long, it gets to the point that you start to believe the goddamn lies put out there. I know this firsthand.

Forgettin' that Dillon is still on my phone talkin' to me, I interrupt his stupid ass to say goodbye then hang up. Need to call Daisy quick, so she can reach out to Mary before she does something really bad. I got a horrible feeling deep inside my gut. I've been where Mary is right now. I dial Daisy's number but it just rings then goes to voicemail. I dial again and same shit. Son of bitch, gotta find Jagger's number. I look in my contacts and hit dial. I wait for one then two rings and hear, "Yo."

"Jagger, it's Griffin, dude. I need your help, bro. Is Daisy around? Need her to reach out to Mary 'cause your ex-bitch has been goin' at her nonstop for the last day or so on social media. Feeling like Mary is gonna do something, I can feel it, bro. Please, Jagger, can I talk to your sister?"

"Hang on a minute, Griffin, we got shit goin' down here too. Let me get to her room, not sure if she is up or not. Give me a minute."

I hear him walking then a knock. A muffled word that I don't catch then a very quiet conversation.

"Dude, I'm back. Daisy, grab your phone, Brat, see if you can get a hold of Mary. It's Griffin on the phone and supposedly the bitch crew is at it again. What? When? You've been gettin' texts from Mary all day today. You been ignoring her. What the fuck, what do they say? Holy shit, no way. Hey, bro, gotta call ya back, hang tight."

Son of a bitch, all I get is nothin'. He hung up on me. Now what? I check my laptop again and see a post from maybe fifteen minutes ago where Mary finally replied back, agreeing that she should just end it. Holy shit, no! God, no. I look around for my keys, not knowin' what I'm gonna do but gotta do something. Goddamn it, what is wrong with these fuckin' mean-ass bitches? My mom would kill me if she heard my thoughts, but these girls are demons with hair and makeup. Runnin' out of the house, I don't even have time to leave a note for my mom. My gut tells me something horrible is about to happen. Need to try and stop it, no matter what. Fuck!

Driving, I again reach out to Jagger 'cause I only have an idea where Mary lives. He picks up on the first ring.

"Griffin, think you're right. Daisy checked her phone and Mary has been sending texts for almost two days. And each one is soundin' more desperate. Daisy has been trying to call her, but Mary's phone is dropping right to voicemail. Where the fuck are you, dude? I hear all kinds of shit in the background?"

"I'm stopped on Center Street by a goddamn train. Ask Daisy where Mary lives. Jagger, we got to make sure she's okay. Again, don't have a good feelin'. Trust me, dude my gut is never wrong."

As I wait for this fuckin' train to pass I can hear Jagger speakin' with Daisy. She's sounding more and more stressed as she tries to find the address. I hear her tell him that she wants to go to Mary's house too. He is arguing with her about it not bein' a good idea. I can see the end of the train so I start screaming into my phone.

"For Christ's sake, how long does it take to find an address? You're wastin' precious time. Give me the goddamn address now."

Hearin' someone running, Jagger is back on the phone, givin' me what I want. Before I can say a word, he drops the bomb.

"Dude, we're closer so gonna check on her. Daisy is gonna go either with me or walk there herself. I'll see ya there."

The gates go up as I hear the silence on the other end of the phone. Driving like a maniac, which I promised my mom I wouldn't do since the last ticket, I fly through lights and stop signs. *Gotta get to Mary* is all that's running through my head.

I turn off of Douglas Street onto High Court, knowing her house is like three blocks down. I hit the stop sign doin' a California stop, quickly going through. Hearing sirens, I look behind me to see a fire truck and ambulance right behind me. I pull to the side to let them pass then see Jagger's car behind them. I start prayin' they are going to pick up some old dude who has had a heart attack not a confused as fuck, young teenage girl doing the unimaginable. Seeing them stop a block ahead, my gut tightens as they jump out and run up a sidewalk to a home with a man in front waving his arms.

Watching the addresses, I see that where they are going in is the address Jagger gave me. Fuckin' shit, we're too late. Mary, goddamn it. Why did you listen to the motherfuckin' bitch demons? Pullin' my car in, I see Jagger right behind me. Before he even puts his car in park, Daisy is out and running toward the house. Behind Jagger a truck pulls in and I see Des and Dee Dee inside. Motherfucker, this is gonna turn into a huge shitshow, for Christ's sake.

Daisy is talkin' to the man who, as I get closer, I can see his shirt is covered in blood. Knowing that can only mean one thing I start to run, just as I see Jagger puttin' his feet to the pavement. More sirens and two police cars now are pulling up. Reaching the front sidewalk, the man is trying to hold Daisy from going in as tears are running down his face. Before I can reach her, Jagger pulls his sister to him. Her back to his front and he holds her tight. Tears and snot are on her face as she loses control, leaving Jagger to adjust and hold all of her weight.

Des grabs the man, pulling him off to the side, his arm around Mary's dad's shoulders that are shaking uncontrollably. I watch Des pull him tight and just give him silent support. I hear something so I look up to see a stretcher being pushed out with Mary on it. Two paramedics one on either side, rushing toward the ambulance. An IV has been started and I can see both of her wrists have been wrapped in some serious gauze. Still, I can see the pink seeping through. She fuckin' cut her wrists. Closing my eyes, I pray she cut them horizontally not vertical.

Hearin' Jagger swear, I look his way to see him trying to hold Daisy up as she struggles to get away and follow the stretcher. I rush over and grab her from his arms, pulling her close. At first she struggles against me, but then all the fight leaves her and she falls into me, arms wrapped around my waist, hangin' on for dear life.

I do the only thing I can. Hang onto her for dear life also.

CHAPTER FOURTEEN

DES

Sittin' in the emergency room, I feel something and look up to see two little kids and their dad, I'm guessin', staring at me. Why the fuck are they gawking at me? I look down and see all the blood on my shirt. Son of a bitch, didn't realize when I had Joe in my arms he was covered in his daughter's blood. No wonder I was gettin' major stink eye from the dad.

Trying to ignore the added attention, I pull Dee Dee closer to me and feel her arms wrap tighter around my waist. Damn, not sure how we're gonna get our girl through this tragedy. All I can do is pray that the girl, Mary, makes it. Otherwise, I know for sure our Daisy will be lost to us. Looking around I see her sittin' between Jagger and Cadence's kid brother, Griffin. She looks like she's in shock, which I'm sure she might be. Seeing what the kids saw today is a parent's worst nightmare.

Joe and his wife, Melody, are tryin' to hold it

together but as each minute goes by you can almost see their hope leaving them. If I remember right, Mary has older siblings in college. So she's the baby all around. Joe catches my eyes, and damn, the pain and agony in his eyes is fuckin' killing me. I don't have anything to give him except my support.

Hearin' the sliding door open yet again, we all look that way to see a physician walking into the waiting room. Feeling like someone just walked over my soul, we hang back, giving Mary's family some privacy. I see the doctor motion to the room off to the side at the same time I feel Dee Dee tightly grab my hand. Not that I do it a lot but enough, so I start prayin' for a miracle.

Watching the family follow the doctor I again look to Daisy, whose eyes also are on the doctor. She looks so tiny between the two young men. Again, another thing on her fragile shoulders and we haven't even dealt with the current shit. Not sure, but thinkin' our plates are full. We need to get our girl on the right path before we are sittin' here for her. That would gut me and kill her mom.

Mary's parents haven't come back yet and not knowin' if that's good or bad news the doctor is deliverin', the waiting is fuckin' killing me. I feel Dee Dee tense up right before she speaks.

"Des, this isn't good. No matter what happens, I have a feeling this is gonna mess up Daisy more than she already is. She's definitely keeping that appointment with Trinity's therapist. Once we find out what's happening with Mary, let's head home so we can continue with our talk with Daisy and Jagger. Can't let any of this go any further. We're in serious trouble, Des. Our family is falling apart and we didn't even know any of this. How can this happen? And when I think like this, I feel guilty because Joe and Melody are waiting to hear news about Mary. God, I never want to go through what they are right now."

Before she can say another word, Joe and Melody come back toward us and I can see both of them have been crying. Joe has his arm around his wife but to me it looks like he is holding her up.

I glance at Jagger and he gives me a chin lift, then turns to both Daisy and Griffin saying something, then all three stand and head our way. Once they arrive, we all turn to Mary's parents as they approach our small group. Joe clears his throat then takes a moment to try and gather his thoughts.

"Well, um, the doc said that we're lucky 'cause if Melody hadn't found Mary when she did, our girl would have died. She's lost a lot of blood and is in and out of consciousness, but they think she will recover. She's going to be staying for a night or two then we've opted for some inpatient treatment. When Mary was brought in, they did an assessment and looked for any other wounds. They found some cuts on her thighs that are partially healed and an infected one under her arm. And she has many scars we had no knowledge of. Feeling really stupid right now. Our baby girl has so many issues going on, we have to get her some professional help. We want to thank you for being here for us. Once she's in a room only family is allowed to see her. And once she's inpatient, not sure how that works at all, we can't even see her in the beginning. Again, you have our gratitude for caring enough to be a support to our family at this time."

Feeling the vibe, I can tell Joe and Melody are at their wits' end. Looking around I catch both Jagger and Griffin's eyes and give them a shrug toward the exit. Then I squeeze Dee Dee's hand before I look at Mary's parents.

"Joe, Melody, no need to thank us. We have ya backs, no matter what. The kids and Dee Dee are headin' out. I'm gonna take your coffee orders and run to pick you up some coffee and food. Gotta keep your strength up. Then I'll head out. Please know how serious I am when I tell ya we're here if either of you need anything. Just reach out and one of us will be here immediately."

They both nod then the goodbyes start. I stand off to the side watchin' everyone trying to get out of a shitty situation quickly.

CHAPTER FIFTEEN

DAISY

After we leave the hospital mom, Jag, Griff, and I walk toward the elevator to the parking lot. With Des doing a coffee run, Mom needs a ride home. I feel out of it, like my body is there but that's it. I hear them talking but can't catch one single word of their conversation. Why did Mary try to take her life? I get being beat down and feeling like everything is black, but crap, to actually do what she did. I'm so much in my head, must not have heard my name called. Next I feel a hand low on my back, which causes me to jerk back. I lift my head to see everyone watching me closely but it was Griff whose hand was on my lower back.

"Lil' Flower, want a ride home? Or would you rather go with Jagger and your mom? Just let me know what ya want."

"Griff, how did you know Mary needed help? I know she wouldn't have texted or called you, so how are you more in the know than us girls?"

Griff stares at me like I have two heads for some reason. I can almost hear his wheels turning in his head. I'm so confused because I can't even comprehend how he would be a part of this. Unless, God tell me I'm wrong, he is part of the bullying group and suddenly got a conscience.

"Get that thought out of your head, Daisy, no way have I've been part of that group of asshole bullies. Dillon called, told me how Sabrina and those bitches were after Mary on her social media. I just had a feeling, so I put a shout out to Jagger and the rest is history as they say. No matter what ya think of me, Flower, I would never intentionally hurt anyone. Not in me, 'cause I've been in Mary's shoes myself."

Immediately I feel like such a loser to even have those thoughts in my head. God, I knew from Cadence and Trinity that Griff was a good guy. Not sure all that happened to him when he was young, but have heard over the years that he was also a victim of bullying and abuse. I've never asked questions of the Powers, as that's his story to tell if and when he wants to. Not sure how to even try to apologize to him for having such nasty thoughts. I put my head down and go down the road I always do when uncomfortable. Avoidance.

"So, Daisy, yes or no to a ride home?"

Before I can even reply, I hear both Mom and Jagger chuckle. Then I hear Mom clear her throat, so I look up at her to see her glancing between Griffin and me.

"Griffin, if you wouldn't mind, can you drive Daisy

home? I'm going to do a quick stop at the grocery store with Jagger. By the time you guys get there Des should also be getting there shortly after. Thinking my girl has had enough for today, don't need to be trudging through a grocery store with her momma."

Then to my utter surprise she winks my way. Holy crap, what universe am I in? Am I imagining this or is Mom trying to hook Griff and me up? And just saying, she isn't being sneaky at all. I look from her to Jag, who is grinning huge. Hating to but my eyes finally land on Griff and he also has an enormous smile on his gorgeous face. Well, who am I to disappoint my family when they are trying so hard on my behalf?

"Sure, Griff, I could use a lift. Mom's right, not in the mood to walk around a grocery store, so maybe we can go through a drive-through and get a coffee, tea, or something."

He nods. Then grabs my hand as I say my goodbyes to both Mom and Jag. I need to get away from the hospital right now. Feels like there are a zillion bugs crawling all over my skin. I'm starting to get the itch to start cutting to relieve the constant and overwhelming thoughts running through my head.

Griff seems to understand as he leads me through the hospital, out the door, and to his car without saying a word. He lets go of my hand and opens the passenger door, giving me a gentle shove in. He waits for me to get settled before he shuts the door. I watch him walk around the front of the car to the driver's side, get in, and settle. I feel his eyes on me so I twist to look his way. The gentle look in his eyes warms me in a way I've never experienced before. He reaches over, lifting my hand in his giving it a squeeze.

"Flower, how ya doin'? I know this has to be fuckin' difficult but know I'm here if ya need help to get through this shit. Together with Jagger and your girls, we will help Mary. She won't be a victim but a survivor. Stay positive, Daisy, 'cause that is the only way to be. Okay?"

I continue to stare in his direction without saying a word. Time seems to pass while we look into each other's eyes, sharing something I have no words for. I feel no pressure from him, it's like he is somehow lifting the burden off my shoulders and taking it on himself. Trying to relieve me of the constant hurt, especially now that I've let my new friend down. Even with all the constant voices in my head telling me what a failure I am, another sound way in the back is also telling me that life is what we make it, like Mom is always preaching. And Griff is right, I have to be strong so I can help Mary when she needs it the most. While I'm processing everything going through my brain, he just sits and waits.

'Thanks, Griff."

Not sure what else to say, I try to look away but he won't let me. It almost feels like he can read into my thoughts deep to my darkest secrets. As I shift my eyes back and forth, he sits in his car, holding my hand, not asking for anything in return. Just being there in the moment with me. With him right there I can feel my body fighting back against the ever-present vibes that usually send me over the edge. The same edge that leads to me eating and vomiting or cutting. But for some reason those feelings seem to be simply disappearing. And without a word from either of us.

After what seems like hours, but is probably just a couple of minutes, Griff reaches down, squeezing my hand, then releases it and starts up his car. He backs out and heads in the direction of my home, without any explanation on how he is able to figure me out. My deepest thoughts have no defense it seems with him around. I lean back against the seat and close my eyes. I'm so tired and feel totally exhausted. Also know once we get home he'll want to talk. Not to mention when my family arrives, they will want to continue our conversation of earlier. Nothing has changed, just gotten pushed back. And I have no idea on what I'm going to say or do. I'm beyond even giving it any thought. So I let the car's rhythms pull me under to a much-needed nap.

CHAPTER SIXTEEN

GRIFFIN

Driving around, trying to think up what to do next, I glance to my right and see Daisy's out like a light. God, she looks so innocent sitting there. Knowing the next couple of days are gonna be friggin' harder than hell on her, I try to come up with a way to be there for her. Nothing comes to mind. I'm drawing a blank and that's not what she needs. Daisy needs someone to give her some direction, not only with Mary's attempted suicide but with all that's going on with her. She appears to have lost even more weight, which she definitely can't afford. Her coloring is also off and the black circles under her eyes tell me that she's not gettin' enough sleep. I'm really worried about her.

Jagger and I have gone over what we can assume is goin' on with her, but it's just a guess. We have nothing concrete yet. He's been watching her like a hawk and has let me know that she isn't eating enough for a damn bird, let alone a human being. Well, that is something we'll touch on later when her parents and brother show up. Now that their eyes are open, they need to nip this in the bud as they say. I spoke to my brother, Cadence, and my sister-in-law, Trinity, and they both agree that Daisy needs to get into therapy as soon as possible. The longer she waits the more the fucked-up shit in her head can take over. Knowing my family's history, I totally get how bullshit can mess ya up.

Hearing her sharp intake of breath, I once again glance that way to see her looking around confused, probably not sure what's going on. Her face shows her internal struggle to wake up, even as her body seems to push deeper into the leather seat she's in. I remember back in the day when I was in therapy, they told me that we have a fight-or-flight response when traumatized. In the beginning I didn't believe a word they said. Never thought they were right or that my life would ever get better. But with time and some very intense counseling, I came around to realizing that life is what you make of it. That you can't change your past but you do have the ability to control your future. I need to share with Daisy and hope that she gets it. She's lucky because I only had my mom at the time. She gave up everything for me when it all came out. Daisy not only has her mom, Des, and Jagger but the entirety of the Horde. That type of support can only help, I think.

Seeing her concern across her face, I think fast then grab her hand.

"Daisy, wanna stop at Dairy Queen to get a

blizzard before we head to your house? I could use some junk food therapy. Whatcha think?"

She blinks slowly then lowers her eyes then her head. I wait for it, knowin' she is gonna blow. She doesn't make me wait too long. The anger and frustration that crosses her face makes me want to laugh but I don't. Can't have a wildcat on my hands.

"Really, Griff, Mary is fighting for her life and you want to go and get ice cream? What's wrong with you? How does that help her fight for her life? And I've mentioned to you before I'm on a diet, why in God's name would I want to go and eat something so fattening as ice cream? Not everyone is blessed with a great metabolism like you Powers guys. Do you not listen when people talk?"

I glare at her, knowing she is trying to piss me off. That way she won't need or want my offering of ice cream. I bet she hasn't eaten anything in a while. And who doesn't think ice cream is the shit? By the looks of her she's still starvin' herself. Son of a bitch, it needs to stop right now.

"Lil' Flower, I get you're worried about Mary, but don't think you can throw that kind of attitude my way and I'm gonna let ya get away with it. We both know shit's about to hit the fan and you're doin' everything you can to continue to spiral down that rabbit hole. I can't let ya, Daisy. So let's try this again, do you want some ice cream or not?"

She glares at me then shakes her head. Okay, that's a big no. Well, she's in for a surprise, 'cause I do want some so she can watch me eat it. I pull through the drive-thru and wait my turn. I give her one more chance and I can tell she really wants some but will never admit it to me. A true anorexic/bulimic. She's thinking I'm the enemy. When my turn comes, I pull up lowering my window.

"Hey, can I get a medium Blizzard with Oreo and a kid's twist cone? That's it."

I'm given the amount and drive around. Feelin' her eyes on me, I turn only my head and raise an eyebrow.

"Dang, Griff, you're gonna eat both of those? Crap, that's more calories than I eat in a couple of days. Not fair, but the way of the world. Women always have to work harder for everything than a guy does."

I ignore her sarcasm, pay, then wait for the order to be filled. When the girl passes me the Blizzard, I put it in the cupholder then reach back for the tiny twist cone. I ask and am given some napkins. I pull up just a bit and place the cone in front of Daisy.

"Daisy, this is for you. Eat as much as you can or want. Something ya are gonna have to get is if ya want something, get it in moderation. So take this so I can drive us to your house. Okay?"

Again, I get the stink eye from her, and for a second or two think she might grab the cone and toss it in my face. But eventually as it starts to drip down my hand, she grabs it and a couple of napkins. Wrapping the cone up, she holds it while looking out the passenger window deep in thought. I give her time and continue on the drive to take her home. Jagger has let me know about how long it would take him and his mom to hit the store and get back to their house. I'm killing time so we aren't alone there. And that is for me totally. It kills to be in her company and not be able to actually hold or kiss her. And right now, thinkin' if I tried either, her knee would find my boys immediately. That thought brings a grin to my face. Not to mention what Jagger or Des would do to me.

Not wanting to piss her off any more than she already is, I try to move my thoughts to how her family, including the Horde and myself, are gonna need to help her through this time. Fuck, wish I had some experience with all that she's doing, but guys normally don't eat and puke or cut themselves. I know how it feels to be bullied but also abused. Though my bullying was by adults who got off on the abuse, while Daisy's being beat down by girls her age. Who for some reason feel the need to make themselves feel better by knockin' her down. Hearin' a noise, I look her way to see her little pink tongue come out, licking off some of the ice cream. I say nothin' but still take it as a win. At this point anything she does is a win. I know this for a fact. Been there done it myself.

CHAPTER SEVENTEEN

DAISY

Watching Jag and Griff clown around in our family room, it's like nothing happened today. Not sure how they can act like that or get what Mary did out of their heads, but like Mom always says: boys will be boys.

Turning toward the kitchen, I see her fixing something to eat. Not sure what it could be, her famous chili or maybe a pot of her chicken soup. Honestly, just the thought of either makes me nauseated. That small cone I wolfed down with Griff is sitting right in my throat. It's taking everything in me not to run to the bathroom and throw it up. And the reason I ate it was not to disappoint Griff.

The only good thing, if I can even think those words, from what happened with Mary is I got out of the *talk* with the family. It was getting pretty deep. I know big mouth Jag was about to go into details on my entries in my diary. On that thought I think I feel something wet on my upper thigh, so quietly tell Mom

I'm gonna go to my room for a minute and head down the hall. After last night and squeezing all that pus out, I'm hoping the cuts will start to heal. Last thing I need is more drama regarding my life and all my problems.

Closing my bedroom door, I hit my bed, dropping my yoga pants before I sit my butt on the edge. Focusing down, I take in a deep breath because it looks even worse than last night. My entire thigh is extremely ruby red up high. The cut closest to my inner thigh has a ton of crap oozing out. Crap, just looking at it my stomach turns. And then taking a breath in, I'm not sure but something smells and I didn't notice it until I dropped my pants. Great, just what I need, a frigging infection. Another thing for everyone to ride my ass about because I'm going to have to tell Mom.

Grabbing my phone, I look up infections online and after scrolling a bit an article says to use hydrogen peroxide on the infected area. So naturally I get up and go to the bathroom I share with Jag. I know there is all kinds of crap under the sink from his many injuries during all of his years in sports. I see a brown bottle in the back and YES, just what I need. Reaching in, I pull it out and sit on the toilet after putting the seat down. Squeezing the cut first, a bunch of yellow crap comes out so I wipe it with some toilet tissue. Opening the bottle up, I pour the peroxide directly on the cut. Immediately it starts to bubble, which I remember from when Mom did it to Jag. What I don't remember is him crying because it hurts so bad. My eyes instantly water as the cut burns and then starts to throb and tingle. I stop pouring for a minute and mop up the stuff on the floor. Then after a couple of minutes, once the fizzing and bubbling stops, I again pour more on the cut. Son of a gun, that is extremely sensitive. I press my hand with a tissue over the cut, trying to apply some pressure to make it hurt less. Instead, it starts to throb, burn, and tingle more, so I remove my hand and glance down to see the tissue covered with blood and guessing pus. Crappity crap. I'm gonna have to keep a close eye on this so it doesn't get worse. Don't want to, but might need to have Mom take me to see the doctor because my entire thigh is really hot and hurts pretty bad.

Bringing the brown bottle into my room, I place it on the floor next to my bed so I remember to use it a couple of times a day. I lay my head on my pillows, closing my eyes for minute, just trying to enjoy the quiet. Lately even when I'm alone I hear white noise, which worries me because even I know that makes no sense. Not to mention I'm always anxious, nervous, and ready to jump out of my skin. Between my stomach always hurting, my thigh constantly reminding me it's messed up, my hair falling out, and being so depressed and sad, guess I can figure why my life totally sucks. Also, in the last couple of months my period just went away. I looked it up on the internet and that can be a 'symptom' of not eating and losing a lot of weight in a short timeframe. That's not a bad thing, not having a period, my mind's smart mouth says in my head.

Not only do I hear buzzing all the time, there's even times like this in the absolute silence my mind can't shut down. Now I'm answering some of my own questions. And that's not good. I remember being little and Mom saying that you have problems if you talk to yourself and bigger ones if you answer your own questions. And sleep is a struggle, either I can't seem to drop off, or literally, I hit the pillow and pass out and struggle to wake up. Thank God my bladder is good or I would be messing my bed whenever my body seems to zone out, not just falling asleep.

Sucks to be me. Immediately I think it does and doesn't. Thinking of poor Mary makes me realize my life isn't that bad. Well, in my eyes it is, but I'm not stuck in a psych ward with people watching and analyzing my every thought and any movement of any sort. Mom has talked with Mary's mom and dad for an update. From what Mom told Des, the professionals are trying to regulate medication to help Mary. Turns out she has severe anxiety and some psychological thing, can't remember the name. So add to all of that the crap from Sabrina and her *biotches* on brooms, it would be too much for anyone, but especially someone like Mary and her issues.

Reaching over to my nightstand I grab a new notebook/journal, opening it to the first blank page. Dang, it's been way too long. I'm still pissed at Jag for grabbing the one that I was writing in. He didn't need to see my darkest thoughts. Maybe this will help, writing stuff down. Seemed to give me a little of comfort in the past. Grabbing a pen, I start to doodle as

I try to get my thoughts together to put on paper. So much has happened, not sure where to begin.

After a few minutes the words seem to flow from me as I fill page after page. The wall has fallen down and dang if I'm not walking through it. Feeling like I've been writing for say fifteen minutes or so, I glance toward my clock and can't believe an hour and a half has passed. After I place my pen on the desk, I lean back on my bed and just be still. Somehow, I managed to find a brief moment of peace of mind. So closing my eyes I take a deep breath, release, and repeat. After doing this for a bit, my head feels lighter and I finally fall into a deep sleep.

CHAPTER EIGHTEEN

DEE DEE

Stirring my chicken soup, my head is completely overwhelmed with everything that has happened today. How can a girl Daisy's age have so much *crap* in her head that she feels the only way to handle everything is to try and kill herself. Just remembering all the blood on Melody makes me shiver. God, just the thought if Mary's mom had stopped for a coffee or got caught by traffic, the ending of this day could have been even more tragic.

Glancing up, I see both Jagger and Griffin sitting on the sectional, talking quietly. Not sure, but just by their body language, the conversation is pretty intense. Jagger's hands are moving in all directions, which is a clear sign that he is very troubled. He used to do that as a small child. Especially after any violence in our home done by his dad. I've never given it much thought but maybe back then had more impact on the kids than I could even image. When their father finally left, I reached out to a women's abuse clinic and they provided us with some counseling. Only my head wasn't in the right place, with all the crushing worry of what was going to happen to the three of us. It never occurred to me that one or both of my kids needed more help. The abuse was never hidden. It was right in their faces. As Jagger got older and bigger he tended to get more involved to try and protect me, which resulted in injuries including bruises, black eyes, fat lips, and even a sprained wrist. He tried his hardest to protect both Daisy and me. To this day I get so furious and disgusted with myself for not leaving sooner. The night their father left, something broke in me. Seeing him beating on both of the kids shattered something in me that has never healed. Jagger also lost his control. When he picked up that bat, my heart was in my throat as he beat his father to a pulp. When the abusive coward got out of Jagger's reach, he made it to the door and ran like the gutless a-hole that he was. I know Des and the guys from the garage had something to do with my husband never showing his face again. I never asked what they did, but for whatever was done I will be forever grateful.

Shaking my head, pushing all those memories to the back of my mind, it hits me we never finished our talk with Daisy. Yeah, I was very upset with Jagger for going through his sister's room, but on the other hand, I'm relieved that we now have an idea of what has been bothering her for so long.

Hearing the garage door going up tells me Des is

finally home. Levi, our dog, is barking like a lunatic, as he always does. I think to myself that I thought he would have been home much sooner. But I'm sure he wanted to make sure Joe and Melody were in a good way before he left. The dominant, alpha male and caregiver, who always wants to handle everything. Turning to greet him, I see him bent over rubbing Levi's wiggling body. When he stands the look on his face immediately makes the hair on the back of my neck tingle. He glances around the kitchen and where the boys are sitting. Then he looks directly at me.

"Sugar, where is Daisy? How's she doing?"

"Des, yeah, she's in her bedroom. Been in there for maybe a couple of hours. Figured she needed some time alone to process everything that has happened. What's wrong? I can see it in your eyes. Please tell me, Des, you're not only freaking me out but scaring me to."

Hearing the panic in my voice, Jagger glances toward the kitchen first at me then Des. He also sees something because he instantly gets up, moving into the kitchen with Griffin following closely behind him. We all look to Des and wait.

"Fuck, not sure how to even say this. When you left, I ran out and got some coffee and food for Joe and Melody. When I got back, they were huddled together, Joe holding his crying wife. Got to say I didn't want to hear out loud what I thought they were gonna tell me. Anyhow, I approached them both. When Joe saw me, he stood, coming my way. I put the coffees and bag of food down as he pulled me off to the side. It took him awhile to get his shit together enough to even fill me in. He asked me if I knew the girls' friend, Agnes. Guess she's also new at the school and is one of the kids that group of bitches has been bullying. He told me he thought she's been here to our house and was a nice kid."

Looking at Des, I shake my head 'cause I'm not sure if I remember her. When Daisy has all the girls over there are so many of them and they keep including more and more. Not to mention Daisy hasn't been as open lately. Clearing his throat Des continues on with his story.

"Joe told me that they were waiting for Mary to be moved to a room when they saw Agnes' parents walking their way. God, Dee Dee." The devastation on his face as he explains what Joe had shared with him makes the hair on my neck stand up. "Joe told me that Melody knew Betty, Agnes's mom, so they thought they were there to give them support because they heard about Mary. 'What a mistake,' Joe said. When they reached them, George pulled his wife close and Joe could see him struggling not to break down. Then both George and Betty looked at Melody and Joe anguish on their faces. Then Joe told me Betty began telling them the worst part of the nightmare.

"Betty asked Melody if Mary was okay. When Melody started to explain about Mary, George interrupted her abruptly, asking them if we had any idea what the girls were up to. Long story short, Dee Dee, Agnes and Mary were both having problems and didn't share with their parents. Instead they decided to make a pact together. Betty found a letter in Agnes' jacket when she went to do laundry. It was a suicide letter to both of them. Their daughter explained what she'd been going through, how alone she felt, and that the bullying was too much for her to handle yet again. Agnes went on to talk about how happy she was to have found Daisy and that whole group of girls. Unfortunately, it was too late because she and Mary had already made their plans together."

Hearing this, I gasp looking at Des then the guys. From the looks on the boys' faces, I figure they have the same thoughts I do. Des continues on.

"From what George gathered from the letter both Mary and his daughter had had enough and couldn't take it any longer. And just to say, it was much worse than any of them knew. The bullying was constant in school, out of school, online, and with all that social media shit. The girls never got a break. So, they decided together to end it all. It happened today because of all the shit that was being posted. They talked and figured now was as good of a time as any. Mary cut her wrists while Agnes found some old pills and took them all. Betty found her in the bathroom seizing. She's in intensive care, on life support."

He looks at me with such pain in his eyes I catch my breath.

"They don't think it's looking good for her, Dee Dee. Fuck, how does this even happen? Is it that bad being a teenager? For motherfuckin' sake."

I move close to Des, my head to his chest. The room is eerily quiet. I'm guessing no one knows what to say. Then Jagger asks the question.

"Des, you say she's in ICU, what does that even mean? Is Agnes gonna be okay? Life support is really bad, isn't it?"

I feel Des's body get tight and he takes in a deep breath. Hearing and feeling this, I try to prepare myself for what's coming next.

"Jagger, all I know is what Joe said George told him. Agnes's dad said the kind and number of pills Agnes took has the doctors worried. And the fact that she wasn't found as quickly as Mary was. She had to be intubated because she wasn't breathing on her own. They are watching her closely and her parents were told the next twenty-four to forty-eight hours are critical. Betty told Melody they were approached by hospital staff, asking if Agnes was an organ donor and would they consider it if things took a turn. George lost it after his wife told us that. So after a day from hell, we now get to tell Daisy that a friend of hers might not make it through the night, while her other friend is in for a long road to recovery."

I look up to see Des's eyes wet. Knowing he would hate to show his emotions in front of the boys, I grab his hand and lead him to our bedroom. Even before the door shuts, he leans against the wall, shoulders moving, hands to his face. Seeing him this way breaks my heart.

"Des, come sit down. I know, honey, please let's sit."

He follows me to our bed and we both take a seat. I say nothing, just hold his hand in mine while he tries to process all the events of today. When he seems like he has it together, I squeeze his hand.

"What do you need from me? Just tell me, I'm here for you, babe."

He stares down at me and I see the shattered look in his eyes, and it hits me in the face. It's not just the two girls and what happened today. My man is imagining what if Daisy would have been part of the pact and gone down that path. How would we all handle the agony those two families are going through?

"Honey, hey, look at me. We got Daisy, don't go there. What we have to do is break this news to her somehow."

Des looks at me for barely a second, before I'm pulled onto his lap and in his arms and held closely to him. I can feel his heartbeat against my ear on his chest. I grab on and hold on for dear life. He needs me and I'm here.

Before I can say a word, I hear the doorbell. *Crap, now what*, I think to myself as Des gets up and out the bedroom, probably to see who it is. Hearing voices, I head out of our room to see what next horrific thing is going to happen today.

Entering the family room, I see Cadence, Trinity, and lil' Hope. Griffin has his niece in his arms, throwing her up in the air as she screams with joy. I watch for a minute or two at how innocent and happy Hope is. How can our kids have gone from that moment in their lives to what is happening with Mary and Agnes?

Not paying attention, I actually jump and let out a shriek when Des touches my arm.

"Sugar, they stopped by to show support to Daisy. They also know that if anyone can cheer her up it's Hope. Mind if I ask them to stay for supper?"

Since I always make a huge pot of soup, I have no problem with this, so just nod my head. As the guys settle on the sectional by the fireplace, Trinity and I are at the island.

"Dee Dee, what's wrong? Is Daisy doing okay? You know you can talk to me. I'm always here if you need me."

I turn looking at the young woman whose pregnancy is becoming very apparent and who has a heart of gold. I smile at her, trying to find the words to explain what a day from hell we've had.

"Trin, there's been one thing after another today. The bullying at that school has hit an all-time high and it pushed two new girls to try and kill themselves. One her mom found in time, the other, it's not looking good. We just found out about the second one, Agnes, when Des got home from the hospital. I'm struggling with how to tell my daughter. We started today with a family talk, which wasn't going too well, then Griffin called Jagger letting him know about Mary. We all headed over there and oh my God, Trinity, my heart breaks for her parents. This one action has definitely changed their lives. From what I gathered, Daisy and her friends were attempting to bring Mary and Agnes into their little group. We found out that they've all been bullied by the same mean girls all through junior high, and it has continued into high school. Jesus, what am I going to do? How do I help my daughter when I have no idea how?"

Trinity stands, coming toward me, pulling me up and into her arms. The unconditional love surrounds me, and not expecting it, my emotions get the best of me and before I know it tears are running down my face. When Trin realizes what's happening she just holds me tighter. I'm so blessed to have the Horde in our lives.

After much discussion, we decide it's best if Trinity and I go to Daisy and break the news about Agnes as gently as possible. So now I'm in my daughter's room to wake her up. I softly approach her bed, sit at the edge, and just watch her sleep. When did she grow up and become a young lady? How did I not see the struggles she was fighting? Why didn't she come to me for help? These questions and many more are running through my head. I'm sure the same questions are in Melody's and especially Betty's. Looking at Trinity, she nods and puts her hand on my back.

Leaning down, I put my hands on Daisy's shoulders, massaging them. She always insists that she's a light sleeper, but every time I try to wake her up it's like fighting with a hibernating bear. Letting her shoulders go, I run my hands up and down her arms, squeezing and hoping to get a reaction. I see her eyes trying to open so I continue what I'm doing until she manages to open her eyes, looking at me. Her eyes get big as she keeps watching me, probably because something must show on my face. She instantly sits up, almost knocking me off the bed.

"Mom, what's wrong? Oh God, did something else happen to Mary? Oh God, please don't tell me Sabrina and her mean girls pushed someone else to do what Mary did? Mom, please talk to me."

As she struggles to catch her breath, I pull her close to me, wanting to protect her from what is about to happen but knowing I can't. It's the dark part of our lives. There are the happy times of life: pregnancy, birth to growing up, becoming an adult and finding your place in the world, and finally when the end comes. Yep, birth...life...death. The circle of life. I just wish my daughter didn't have to experience it all in one day.

CHAPTER NINETEEN

DAISY

Not sure how I know but I can feel it. My stomach hurts, as does my head. I feel like someone beat me up and probably would have slept all afternoon. But with Mom and Trinity here, waking me up, then gently guiding me out of my room into the family room, I know something is up. They place me between Jag and Griff, who are on the love seat. They both put a hand on each of my knees. Des walks up to me, crouching in front of me, Mom right behind him. Trinity reaches for Hope but she gets away, running to me. She actually leaps onto me and I go back on the love seat. As we greet each other, I can feel the doom in the room. When Trinity grabs Hope's hand, leading her to the back screen porch to play with our cats, Vinnie and China, I know shit is about to hit the fan. I feel surrounded by everyone, but not in a bad way. I impatiently wait for Des to tell me what the heck is going on.

"Daisy girl, there's been another incident. No, it's not Mary. She's stable for now, talked to her dad. Honey, I'm sorry to tell you this, but Agnes also tried to hurt herself. No one knew they made a suicide pact together. She took a bunch of pills that were in her parents' medicine cabinet. No one found her for a while and when they did, she had a seizure and her breathing was very shallow. By the time the ambulance got her to the hospital, her heart had stopped twice and they had to intubate her. Not sure you know what that is, but they put a tube down her throat to make sure her body is gettin' the right amount of oxygen. Baby girl, she's in ICU and they aren't giving her parents a lot of hope right now. I'm so sorry, Daisy."

My body is trembling and I can't keep my hands still as I wring them in my lap. My head feels like it's going to blow off my head. Both Jag and Griff squeeze my knees in support, but the scary part is I'm not feeling anything. It's like Des told me the weather took a turn for the worse. I hate this lack of emotions, but right now it's preventing me from losing my mind.

"WHAT...what are they doing for her, Des? What do you mean they didn't know how? Who's they? Did her folks find her? Oh no, both Mary and Agnes have been sending texts the last couple of days, but honestly, I had so much going on I just ignored those texts like I did with all the girls. It's my fault because I wasn't there for them. I was trying to get them into our queen group and when they truly needed me, I bailed. I thought only about myself. Oh my God, all this is happening because of that bitch Sabrina and her mean girl clique. They forced Mary and Agnes to do this. And you, Jag, brought her in our home all summer long. I know what you two were doing in your bedroom when Mom and Des were at the garage. She's evil, Big Brother, how'd you not see that? She needs to go away and be punished. I don't get it though, why is she like that? How can you be so cruel and mean to someone that you force them to take their own life? OH GOD NO, NO, NO, NO, no, no, nooooooo."

Jumping up, I start to pace back and forth. Hearing a God-awful screeching sound that hurts not only my ears but is breaking my heart. Feeling strong arms around me, not sure who it is, but it feels good. Kind of what is holding and grounding my mind right now so it doesn't plunge into the darkness. Trying to catch my breath becomes a struggle. Then I hear Des tell Jag to get my inhaler and I'm kind of dragged to the couch. Someone gives me a gentle shove and I'm sitting down, pulled real close to a warm, hard body. My head is telling me it's Des comforting me and when I look up it's confirmed. Des's face is filled with such concern and worry. As I watch his face, he leans down so our foreheads are touching. We stay like this for a long time. My trembling eventually stops and my head isn't pounding as bad. He always knows what to do.

"So what happens now? Is Agnes going to die? Should I go to the hospital and try to, I don't know what I can do, or maybe be there for her parents? I feel so bad, they're new here, I don't think they have had a lot of time to get to know people."

I look over my shoulder and see Mom, Jag, Griff, and Cadence watching Des and me. Totally forgot the Powers were even here. Guess Trinity is keeping Hope occupied in the back while I lose my ever-loving mind. Mom's arm is around Jag, holding him close. Griff is on Mom's other side, leaning into her. Cadence is on the other side of his brother. Looks like a normal family. For some reason I giggle because what the hell is 'normal' anymore?

"Joe said he would call us if there's a change with either girl or if they need anything. I'm sure Joe and Melody will be there for Agnes's parents. No one knows how they feel more than Joe and his wife. I know we have some unfinished business, baby girl. And before you get your feathers in a ruffle after what happened with Mary and now Agnes, we can't push it off any longer. Jag, go get whatever you wanted to share with us. Griffin and Cadence, know y'all have an idea of what's goin' on, but leavin' it up to Daisy if she wants you guys here."

My head jerks up at Des's words then my eyes move to first Griff then his brother. Both just stare at me for a moment. Cadence gives me a small smile.

"Lil' Flower, your choice. We'll stay or go."

Knowing what's coming, I figure I might as well have it out there. The Horde will know anyway, there are no secrets in our 'family.'

"Thanks for saying that, Griff. It's probably not

going to be pretty and knowing our family talks get very loud, but if you want to stay I'm good with that, I guess. We're like extended family anyway, right?"

He studies me for a minute or two then nods. Cadence approaches me, pulling me into his arms. I always seem to forget that he's so built. God, his arms around me make me think nothing can ever hurt me.

"Daisy girl, you got this. Ya know my history is out there, not sure how much ya know, but if I can work through my fuckin' son of a bitch of demons, not to mention Trinity working hers out. Then we come together and bring children into the mix. Most important thing to remember is you are NOT alone. We all have your back."

Hearing noises like a herd of cattle are in the house, I turn to see Jag walking toward the family room his arms full of stuff. When I look closer, the stuff is all mine. Oh no, he has my journal, my diet journal, and my cutting box. He also brought the peroxide too, not sure why. I head in the direction he is going to and sit down on the corner of the couch, legs up, arms around them. I can feel the pull in my thighs and for some insane reason I need that. To feel something—anything —right now. Don't want any of them close to me while they tear my life apart. I blank my face, even though it feels like a thousand butterflies are in my stomach.

"Daisy, we know you're worried about your friend, but ya need to see how worried we are about you. So even though I agree with your mom that Jagger shouldn't have gone through your room, he felt his reasons outweighed his invasion of your personal space. And, Little Queen, gotta say I agree with his way of thinking. Don't get pissed, Daisy. So gonna give him the floor. We are not attacking you, Daisy, we want to help."

Feeling like I'm going to cry, I breathe deeply and look at the fireplace and not my family. The feeling in the room is weird. Not looking up, I wait for my brother —who I've looked up to all my life—to start the process of tearing my life apart, literally. And when he does, not sure I'll be able to forgive him, no matter what his intentions are. I would never do anything like this to him, no matter what. Yes, I would have his back, but in a way that I wouldn't betray the bond we share together. He's not only my big brother but my best friend too. Well, guess as usual, I have no say so in my life. Sucks being the baby of the family. No control over anything.

CHAPTER TWENTY

JAGGER

Watchin' my kid sister's face, I can almost feel the desperation pouring off of her. Never in my wildest dreams growing up did I think she would end up in this situation, and it would be up to me to try and get her on the right road. A road filled with so much bullshit covering the path it's gonna be very hard, but with all of our help, just maybe we will be able to pull her back before it's too late. Can't or won't even imagine Daisy in Mary's or Agnes's situations.

"Daisy, before we start, got something to say to ya. I really do respect your privacy and if you had given me any other choice, I never would have gone through your shit. I swear, lil' Brat. Sayin' that, my stomach turned readin' the abuse you've been goin' through in school, at home, and in general. I owe ya an apology because if I wasn't with Sabrina, and didn't have her here, you would have at least been safe in your own home. Yeah, Mom and Des, I had her here during the summer when ya both were at work. Don't worry, I was careful and used the condoms that Wolf, Cadence, Gabriel, and you gave me, Des. I ain't stupid. And I know too much information especially for you, Mom, but I'm not a little boy anymore."

Watching Mom's face turn bright red, she literally punches Des in the arm hard. *Damn, didn't know she had that in her*, I think to myself.

"Son, we will be having a conversation about this later. Right now, I can only handle one situation at a time. Des, really? You gave our seventeen-year-old son condoms, along with the other crazy nuts at the garage? What were you thinking?"

I turn to Des, who is lookin' at me like he wants to be anywhere but here at this moment. Not to mention he looks ready to pounce on me and kick my ass. I smirk his way as he literally growls my way.

"Sugar, come on, ain't it better to be safe than sorry? I'm sure you don't want a grandkid right at this moment. We have so much other shit we need to deal with right now that is so much more important, don't you think? Tryin' to be proactive for Christ's sake."

Shaking her head, looking from Des to me, I can tell she's totally pissed at both of us. Well, won't be the first time she's mad or disappointed with me. Turning, I look back at Daisy who has her elbows on her knees, head in her hands. Watchin' her for a minute I'm able to see the pain in her eyes. Fuck, how did I not see it before? Well, could be because my head was up my ass this entire year. Son of a bitch, what an idiot I am.

Thinkin' with the wrong head and not protectin' my sister.

"As I was sayin', I take responsibility for my part in this pile of shit. But, Daisy, we have always had open communication between us. Why didn't ya feel safe enough to tell me? I wish ya would have let me know how bad it had gotten or that you were sufferin' and in pain. Little Brat, I've always told ya, it's you and me against the world. Remember? Even when we were little and the sperm donor was beatin' on Mom and me, I always tried to take care of you. That, sister, will never change, no matter how old we get or where we're at. You're not only my sister but also my best friend, Daisy, and I let ya down. Can't ignore it any longer. Your actions are hurtin' you not only physically but emotionally too. That can't continue. So I'm gonna give ya a chance to explain to all of us why you're doing the bullshit your pullin'. Ya gotta tell them everything, or else I'm gonna. This way it's still your story, I'm just pushing you to tell them before ya was ready. I know you're mad at me, can see it in your face. I'll take that any day 'cause that means you're alive and in my life. So come on, Brat, we only want to help ya, that's all. And ya need help before it's too late. Ya hear me?"

Daisy watches my face the entire time with no emotion at all. Nothing, blank as a canvas an artist is getting ready to paint on. Fuck, don't tell me I didn't get through to her. Don't know what else to do, this can't keep goin' on. Right before I can reach for the diary, Daisy grabs it, holdin' it close to her chest. Her face is pale and her hands are shaking slightly. She's strugglin' to look at all of us, then leans back on the love seat, the journal still on her chest while her eyes skip between the five of us. I sit back down and wait. She has to do this on her own in her time. I can't imagine how hard this has to be for her. Havin' no choice and bein' forced to tell us her deepest secrets. I mean, God Almighty, we all have some secrets that we hope to never have to share with another human being. I know Mom probably hasn't told Des everything that went on with our loser sperm donor, 'cause if she had Des would have killed that motherfucker. Mom doesn't even know I saw one time when that asshole, drunk as a skunk, beat her up then raped her. She told him no and he spit in her face and said she was his wife, she didn't get to say no to him. I carry that guilt with me every day but I was just a little kid, couldn't do anything to help her. And I'm sure that kind of shit happened all the time to her back then. As I continue to drift back to our past, I hear a throat clear. Lookin' up I see Daisy opening up her diary and looking through the beginning of it. Okay, maybe she is gonna get on board and grab this shitty situation by the balls. She has to start talking and about everything, can't leave anything out. I rather she give her story to everyone than me piecemeal it together. If I have to, she will never forgive me, I know that. After I gave it some thought, that's how I came up with idea of givin' her an option. Might make her feel like she's regained some of her control.

"Jag's right, need to get off my butt and try to

explain why my life seems to be falling apart. The counselor at school suggested I do this awhile back, after the situation at school but I just ignored her at first then lied, telling her that I was starting to feel good enough to share with my family. She wanted me to tell you in my own words, because it's supposed to give me some of my power back. I don't have a clue how to start. Please give me another minute or so to try and gather my thoughts. I'm going to start at the very beginning, which isn't recent. When I was little and before Des came into our lives. I think that was what started my spiral into this black hopeless hole I call my life. It festered until I couldn't handle it. Should have told you, Mom, or you, Jag, how I was feeling but was just so scared. Feels like I've been afraid all my life from one thing or another. It just seems like each day more and more crap got dumped on my plate and before I knew it, felt like I was drowning.

"I have my queens, and in the beginning we would share our sad lives with each other. Some of us thought it would make our lives easier, and we wouldn't get picked on so much, say if we could lose weight. Amethyst's older sister was bingeing then purging and told us about how she lost a ton of weight, so we all decided to try it. Well, all five of us started together but Bird and Akiria didn't do it for long. V really got obsessed with it, so much that she started to do other strange and then really disturbing stuff. Not sure you guys know, and you can't say a word, but she ended up in a mental hospital. They had tried to find the right drugs to chemically balance her. So that left only Amethyst and me. We both were losing weight and started getting crazy because the results were showing. So we turned it into a crazy competition between us. The competition got really intense when we started to try to outdo each other. Then Amethyst found her a-hole boyfriend. When she started to pull away from me and the queens because of him, I knew something was up. I confronted her at school one day and she told me that I needed to grow up, can't be a little girl forever. Then she informed me that her and her boyfriend were, you know, doing it and it was great. That's why we couldn't be attached at the hip forever. Also told me I was jealous of how thin she was and because she had that guy in her life. She threw in my face that I didn't have a boyfriend because I was such a good little girl. Later Akiria told me that Amethyst was doing just about everything with her boyfriend. She thought she was going that far to hang on to him, but I don't know. She left our nerd group to experience as she said 'true love.' Well, until she found out that pig of a guy was not only doing her but also two other girls. She had to go to the doctor 'cause she had issues, umh you know, Mom, down below. Her vajajay, if you guys didn't catch it."

I almost bust a gut at Daisy's face, which was gettin' redder by the minute. Fuck those girls are just kids, what guy would be fuckin' with them? If I'm not mistaken that's statutory rape. If I find out that guy is older, he is gonna get introduced to my two friends...

My goddamn fists. Mom just stares at Daisy for a second then carefully puts it out there, honest as ever.

"Sweetie, are you telling us your friend was sexually active? Oh my God, that can't be, you're still little girls for God's sake. Oh no, please tell me you didn't follow in her footsteps. Did peer pressure push you to do something you might be regretting, so now you're punishing yourself? Daisy, hey, please tell me and no matter what I won't be mad."

Daisy, Des, and I are lookin' at Mom like she is crazy. Griff and Cadence are more than uncomfortable. Thinkin' Mom forgot it wasn't just us. Can't believe she called out Brat in front of everyone about shit like that. I don't ever need to know where, what, when, how, and mainly who. The images in my mind make me want to kill someone. The thought makes me fuckin' gag. I feel like I'm gonna puke. Hearin' the same noises across the room, Des has his hand coverin' his mouth face lookin' a bit green. I look to Griffin and his eyes are to the ground, but his face is ruby red. Yeah, my bro has it bad for Daisy, he's so pissed off right now. Before I gauge Cadence's reaction, I hear it softly at first then louder and louder. Holy fuck, we're all on the verge of pukin' our guts out and my sister is giggling hysterically. Are ya kiddin' me?

CHAPTER TWENTY-ONE

DAISY

Once I start, the giggles turned into hysterical belly hurting laughter. And man does it feel good. It was like lettin' the carbonation out of a new liter of pop, when all you hear is the hiss then sometimes the soda foams up and runs down the sides. I'm hunched over, eyes closed, laughing and laughing until I realize I'm the only one. Cautiously, I peek out of one eye from the side to see my family watching me with a mixture of worry, concern, and uneasiness. Mom's eyes are wide and kind of disturbed, while all the guys look green in the face. That makes me laugh harder. Guess the thought of me growing up and engaging in a, well ya know, a sexual situation made them sick to their stomachs. Guess I better put them out of their misery regarding my lack of sexual experiences.

"No, Mom I didn't do something I'm regretting. You taught me better than that, and I know that is something truly special and I shouldn't give it away to just anyone. Can't believe you would even go there."

Watching Mom's face, it turns red then she gives me big eyes at first, then one of her beautiful smiles letting me know she believes me. Thank God, didn't need anything else to worry about in my life right now.

I try to pull it together and get myself under control. I take a deep breath then another until I can control the giggles and laughter that continue to come out, especially after watching Mom's face and big eyes. Leaning back into the sofa, I try to relax and get this crap over with now that my family knows I'm not sexually active. But not sure where to begin or how to truly explain why for some reason hurting and isolating myself, instead of asking for help, is the road I went down. Personally, not sure if our childhood actually has something to do with why my life took a turn. Or if it's peer pressure with my anxiety and mental suffering, can't put my finger on it. Something in my life changed my life path.

As I try to organize my thoughts, everyone grabs their seats again getting comfortable. After a few minutes the utter silence is starting to grate on my already frayed nerves. The overwhelming fear of this exact moment when I have to share everything with them. I run my hands through my hair, shift in my seat, grab my ankle putting it over my other leg, then immediately put it back down. I stand and sit back down, both legs tucked under me until I move my left leg, bending in front of me so I can huddle with my arms and pull it closer to my body. When my fidgeting finally calms down, my head lifts, and first thing I see is my mom watching me closely. Seeing me peeking at her, she gives me a very small hesitant smile. And that and that alone gives me the courage to start this. Finally seeing how much my mom always has my back. Not sure how long I just sit here, mind running all over, while I totally lose focus of the love and support my mom always gives me. That alone tells me the need for some intense counseling in my life, due to the lack of my decision-making lately.

"Okay, I'm gonna try to explain this and where I'm at right now. First, Mom, this isn't your fault. In fact, there is no blame to be placed on anyone, including myself. Since she didn't have any earlier appointments before this coming Monday I've talked to Dr. Hendrix, Trinity's counselor as you know, on a Zoom call and she explained to me that sometimes things happen in our lives that can, I think she used the word alter, our path. I've even read some books on it and a lot of the issues are ones I'm having. So when we were little living with 'dad,' I think seeing all that, something broke in me. All those beatings you took, Mom, and then when he started on Jag, I was so scared knowing my turn was quickly approaching. The feeling of walking on eggshells became a way of life for me at home. No, Mom, no blaming yourself, it was all his fault. He had issues that he never faced. The thought has run through my head that maybe all my anxiety and issues are from HIM. Maybe I got more of him than you.

Then he started the emotional abuse, with the name-calling and saying mean things to me when you guys weren't around. He told me that if I told either of you, he would kill you and then beat the crap out of me. That day Jag walked in, when he was beating me, was one of the first times that he took it that far. After that last fight and he left us, the constant guilt started to eat at me. And as a kid I didn't know how to process and deal with it, so it festered for all these years. Growing up and then the bullying started in junior high, everything came to a head.

"At first, I would hurt myself with pinching, slapping, or even poking needles under my skin. Then one day we were watching a movie, Mom, you probably don't remember, it was about a young hormonal girl weighed down with many problems. She took to abusing herself first with her weight and food then turned to cutting herself. I've watched that movie many times since and the scene of the first cut opened my eyes, making me curious, as sick as that sounds. Took to the internet, I researched everything there is on cutting. Did you guys know there are even social media groups for like-minded people to share their experiences? I joined a couple of them. It was a self-taught, step by step, how to begin and use cutting as a method to relieve your anxiety and stress. I gathered my 'toolbox' of supplies and once I had it, I would take it out over and over just to look at. I convinced myself that all I planned to do was keep the stuff and never use it. Then one day, I think in the middle of eighth grade, after a really rough day at school, came home and no one was here. By then my eating disorder was in full swing so I couldn't drown my sorrows in food, and I pulled out my box just to look at it. I thought, *how hard could it be to maybe cut myself just a little?* I've watched a bunch of self-made videos on YouTube so thought I had the expertise on how and where to cut. First time I was nervous as all hell, oh sorry, Mom. Took out the knife and razor blade, wasn't sure which to use. Cleaned my upper inside thigh then grabbed the razor, fumbling at first, but then put it against my skin. As soon as I saw the blood, it felt like a heavy weight lifted off my chest immediately. So I cut a bit more. The more blood that came out and leaked down my leg, the better I started to feel. Lighter, like my problems were flowing with the deep red blood running down my thigh. For a while it was my secret, but one day my queens and I were sharing our darkest secrets with each other. Yeah, that's what crazy young girls do. One of them shared they already had sexual intercourse, while another spoke about how she didn't understand her parents and their really strange relationship. One was mixing her prescribed medication with booze because she thought she was bi-sexual, and one was struggling with religion and her parents. When it was my turn, I blurted out that I was a *cutter*. When they didn't believe me, I showed them my upper legs, which were covered in tiny scars and cuts in different stages of healing. That night, after sharing my darkest secret, one of them started cutting too. We conspired together and it became again like a contest. Who went the deepest, the most blood, how many times in a night, the list goes on and on."

Hearing a gasp, I glance at Mom to see she has her hand to her mouth, tears running down her face. Des was holding her from the side. See, this is the main reason I didn't want to tell them, because no matter what, it would hurt one or all of them. Shifting, I peek at Jag and the emotions running across his face alarm me for a quick minute. When he sees me looking his way, he gives me a gentle smile. I reach and grab the water, taking a huge gulp, so I don't have to look at the Powers guys, especially Griff who gives me a tight smile that doesn't meet his eyes. By the time I put the water back on the table it is empty. Obviously with my dry mouth I'm talking too much.

Once Mom calms down and everyone again takes a seat, they look expectantly at me. Right at that moment, I decide to give them a shortened version of all this bull crap.

"So besides the cutting I was fighting with body image and my own sense of worth. Then the bullying got really bad. Sabrina and her mean girl clique took every opportunity to physically, mentally, and emotionally beat me up, each and every day. The only place I felt safe was at home. Well, until you brought her here, Jag. No, no, don't take that as me pointing a finger in your face or blaming you at all, brother. You wanted to know my story, so giving it to you. Bro, you had no idea that while you were getting 'busy', Sabrina and her mean girls were tormenting me. Anyhow the more they picked on me, the more time I spent cutting myself. And by this time, I'd not eaten a real meal in so long I couldn't remember. My stomach actually would hurt if I did try to eat. Then noticed some of the cuts weren't healing and looked infected. Tried to clean them up and got lucky that time because eventually they did scab over and heal.

"Then Mary and Agnes came to our school and Sabrina saw new victims. They shifted most of their attention from me to them. And to be honest, I was kind of grateful they were off my back. At first I ignored how they were treating both Mary and Agnes. Then Griff saw them abusing the girls and lost it. Pushed back with no fear. I thought we were making headway but that was before they moved the bullying to social media. And now it's so bad they are both in the hospital. Not sure how Jag knew, but he walked into our bathroom one day while I was cleaning my leg and voilà here we are."

Mom is sniffling then reaches to Des, grabbing his hand.

"Daisy, how bad are your cuts? Do you need to see a doctor? And what do you actually weigh because you look extremely thin? I've tried to talk to you about this and you either went ballistic or silent. Oh shit, why am I acting like this weak-ass woman when my daughter is slowly dying right in front of my eyes? Come here, my sweet girl, please I need to feel you in my arms. Please, Daisy."

I stare at Mom for a minute or two then slowly get up. As soon as I'm within an arm's-length, she pulls me into her. Feeling her arms around me I let out a huge breath. God, I missed this. I truly had forgotten how good this feels. After a few seconds, I sense someone behind me then I feel Jag there, reaching around both of us. I lose it and feel the first of many tears running down my cheeks. Then not sure if it's exhaustion or just plain relief, my body relaxes and I genuinely hold on to my family for dear life. My life. I'm finally starting to feel safe and loved again.

CHAPTER TWENTY-TWO

DAISY

Lying in bed after the 'family conversation' that has me totally exhausted, mentally and physically, I sigh. I gave it all to Mom, Des, and Jag. And don't forget Griff and Cadence. Once I started talking, there was no stopping me for some reason. Definitely a Chatty Cathy for sure. It's like Fern who always says when someone rambles people say, "Who put a quarter in you?"

While answering Mom's million and one questions, I didn't realize that Des had called Gabriel to come over and check out my cuts because Jag said he thought they were badly infected. Of course, Fern came with her husband. Also tagging along was a young guy who had stopped by to visit with the Murphys. I think his name is Cassius Rivera but the Murphys called him 'Doc,' which is hilarious because that's what we all call Gabriel. Guess they met him during the charity ride that was done for Fern when she was fighting cancer. Cassius is part of the Grimm Wolves MC and the whole club came and supported the cause. Both Gabriel and Cassius were medics in the service, so a friendship started and whenever he was in town he would stop and visit, not to mention check in on Fern. When Des called, they thought four eyes were better than two.

Fern and Mom went into the kitchen to get some coffee together so I went and put on some shorts so the 'Docs' had a better view of what I've done to myself. Des never left the room and was holding my hand. Gabriel was so gentle and never once asked any in-depth questions. And the young guy, got to say, man, was he gorgeous. Brown hair and eyes. You can tell he worked out because he was pretty ripped. Heard him telling Des that his dad was failing and you could hear the pain in his voice. Cassius said that someone name Stitch and his ol' lady, Grace, had his dad with them. Guess his dad knew them pretty well.

When the bandage is removed from the one cut, both of them take in a deep breath. I watch as Cassius walks out to get 'something' from his cage, whatever that means. He comes back with a large messenger bag. He starts pulling out vials of stuff, needles, and all kinds of things in sterile packages. I see Des give Gabriel a look which causes him to shrug his shoulders. When Gabriel moves out of the way, I pull back as Cassius approaches me. He gives me a small smile and just waits for me to calm down and chill.

"Daisy, right? All I'm gonna do is flush the infected ones out with some sterile saline. I've got some really strong antibiotics that I can give ya, a shot to help you with the infection. Looks like that shit has been goin' on for a while. No judgment here, girl. I've seen just about everything between bein' in the military and now with the Grimm Wolves MC. I'm there and handle all the injuries, so believe me I can hang with just about anything. Just let me know when ya're ready. Might be a bit painful, not gonna lie, but we don't have a choice, it's gotten too bad. Gabriel will be here to help so if it gets to be too much, just let us know. Hey, Des, can you get some Tylenol for Daisy? I'm out in my bag, damn Iron's been eating them like friggin' candy, the asshole."

Both Des and Gabriel laugh at Cassius's comments. I watch him arrange everything he took out of the bag and place all of it on the table. He then gets up and heads to the bathroom down the hall. Guess he is washing his hands. Before I can say a word, he's back grabbing some gloves as Gabriel now heads down the hallway too. He's gone just a few minutes and then walks right to us, reaching for a pair of the medical gloves. I'm wondering how this biker dude can have all these medical supplies on hand and how he is able to get them. Feeling someone watching me, I look up to brown eyes watching me closely.

"Yeah, I get it, Daisy, but it doesn't matter how I have this shit, just be thankful I do. If not, your parents would need to take ya to the hospital where they would ask a hundred questions and have ya talk to a shrink. Ready? The sooner we get started the quicker we'll be done and you can rest."

I nod and he grabs something in a bottle. I watch both of them work on my upper thigh, neither saying a word. At times I don't think I can take much more but they never stop. The one that was oozing with pus is by far the most painful. Gabriel says something quietly to the biker dude, who nods. Gabriel looks to Des, telling him to get Dee Dee. I start to panic as we wait for Mom to come back in.

She enters with a tray of coffee and cream and sugar things, while Fern has a platter of desserts, I have no idea where they came from. Mom puts the tray on the dining room table and moves quickly to my side.

"What's wrong? Do we need to take Daisy to see a real doctor? Oh crap, didn't mean any disrespect, guys, swear just worried about my daughter."

They both smile at her, and dang again, one really good-looking biker even though he is older than me. He has a leather vest on with something on the back with wolves and stuff. Trying to keep my mind on what's going on, I lean back not on the cute biker. Doesn't make sense as I really like Griff. Maybe I am losing my mind, who knows? Cassius and Gabriel stop for a minute glancing up to the crowd around the room which includes Jag, Grif, and Cadence.

"Okay, gonna lay it out there, ya tell me whatcha want to do. There are two cuts that are really bad. I'm thinkin' they have abscessed and need to be drained, 'cause I'm not gettin' all the shit out and don't want to leave it like it is. If it's okay with ya, we can give Daisy a local and take care of it or you can go to the emergency room. It ain't gonna go away on its own. Only issue I see is the physicians in the ER will ask questions and might have her talk to a shrink. Your choice though, just let me know.

Before Mom and Des can even talk about it, I clear my throat to get everyone's attention.

"If it's okay, Mom, can he just do it here? I don't think I can take much more today, it's been pretty rough, if you know what I mean. I'm not feeling all that good and haven't for a while. Thinking it's the infection. I didn't really take care of the cuts probably like I should have and now I'm paying for it. Cassius, Gabriel, if you think you can fix it, please then go ahead. I'm as ready as I'll ever be."

Feeling someone next to me, I look up just as Griff grabs my hand, holding on tight. Never says a word or looks at me as disgusting, just giving me his support. And for that my heart beats a bit faster as I realize I like him even more because he's such a good guy.

So after everything is done, my legs are wrapped up. Mom offers coffee to all the guys as they start talking military and then bikes, so Mom, Fern, and Trinity—who finally came in from the back porch—go into the other room. That leaves Hope and me, so we both sit down on the floor just talking quietly and really don't do anything except hang out.

The guys are talking about the Horde and garage. Telling Cassius how busy business has been and Des asks him how the club was doing. Half listening, I just chill on the floor with Hope now that the television is on. We are watching one of the princess movies and I must have drifted off because next thing I know, Des is picking me up and carrying me to bed. He places me gently down, looking into my eyes. I can see his concern. He says nothing, drops down giving me a quick kiss and leaves, closing the door softly.

And now here I'm staring at my ceiling, not seeing anything. Feeling so drained and empty but scared to death because now that everything is out in the open, not sure what comes next. With this last thought I again drift off to a deep sleep. Something I've not done peacefully in forever.

CHAPTER TWENTY-THREE

DEE DEE

Checking on my daughter, who is totally passed out in her bed, I head toward Des who is in our room. Jag is in his doorway waiting on me. He reaches down and gives me a tight hug and kiss on the cheek. I hold on for dear life because if not for my son's very eagle-eyed observation of his sister, God only knows how much longer Daisy could manage with all the crap going on. My hand touches his face as I tell him how much I love him. He enters his room as I continue on to where Des is in the doorway, waiting on me, his eyes taking everything in.

Reaching for me, he pulls me in, and closes the door quietly, never letting me go. His arms wrap around me, holding me closely, saying not a word. As usual he knows what I need and I wrap my arms around him, trying to get as close as possible, while allowing his warmth to surround me. We stay like this for a while, then he moves us to the bed, placing me on the edge and sits right next to me. His arms are holding me tightly as he places his head on top of mine. I feel the strength in him as he gives me all the time in the world to absorb everything that has gone down today. I'm so thankful for both of the *Docs,* for taking care of those infected cuts. I vaguely remember the Grimm Wolves MC from the charity ride for the Murphys. They are a rough bunch of bikers who follow their own rules, but were also a huge help. Glad Cassius was around because he sure knew what to do and was stocked up with supplies. I know Daisy was curious, but glad she didn't ask too many questions. Clubs and bikers keep everything close to the chest.

Feeling a bit more grounded, I lean into Des smelling his unique scent. God, I love this man. Always has my back. Even back in the day when I first left the kids' dad. I had no idea how much those years affected Daisy. I'm thinking that is the beginning of her troubles.

"Sugar, don't even go there. All that bullshit is on that jagoff you were married to. He had no right in hell to put his hands on you and the kids. He's lucky we left him alive when you finally left him. The only good that came from our *meeting* is he took us at our word and got the hell out of Dodge, so to speak. Probably helped having Cadence, Wolf, and Gabriel there, along with some of the guys from the garage. So how do you think this all went today? Surprised at all that Daisy shared with us. Gotta say, really fuckin' proud of Jagger givin' his sister some of her power back, lettin' her think she had a choice to tell us what the goddamn hell was goin' on. He's pretty smart for a teenage boy, don't ya think?"

Shaking my head, I realize in this moment how very lucky I am with the kids. After all the disfunction they experienced while they were little kids, they each turned out pretty good. Yeah, Daisy is having a rough row right now, but after today I'm thinking she might be on the right road, even though it's going to be a long one. Going to have to watch her though. And no, she didn't eat a ton of food tonight but she did try. And none of us allowed her to go to the bathroom right after she ate so she could force herself to purge. I know that made her mad, but until we can get her some more professional help with her specific issues, we got to keep our fingers on her pulse, so to speak. After listening to her, I'm thinking that the counselor Trinity recommended might not be enough with all the issues my daughter is dealing with. Daisy is still going to see her on Monday, but Gabriel was going to ask some folks he knows for a recommendation for a therapist that deals with the majority of her issues.

With my mind going in all different directions, I must have not heard Des's question at first 'cause he puts his mouth right next to my ear.

"Sugar, how ya doin'? I know a lot was dropped onto us today. But as I always say, as long as we have each other we can handle any bullshit that comes our way. Right now, we have to focus on Daisy 'cause, darlin', she's at that 'Y' in the road. We can't let her down now that she finally felt safe enough to share with us all about the shitshow goin' on in her life. How we missed so much, don't have a fuckin' clue. Feel like a total asshole 'cause I thought we had a pulse on our kids, but guess not. They both surprise the shit out of me. I also hate to mention it, with all he did for his sister, but we are gonna need to talk to Jagger about what we found out about his 'guest' who came around here after school when we were at work. Don't want to be a total dick, but can't have him disrespecting not only our rules but his fuckin' younger sister. You and I both know that he took it all the way 'cause you found the empty condom packages. I'm kinda pissed at him, especially since I talked to him about the importance of makin' right decisions when thinkin' about sex. Fuck, thank God he used protection with that crazy bitch he was seein'. And yeah, I'm being an asshole but that teenage bitch has made Daisy's life a livin' hell for years. Let me know if we're gonna both talk to him or if you want one or the other of us to do it. I'm good either way. And I know you're kinda pissed at me and the guys for givin' him the condoms but thank Christ we did."

Damn, the crap never ends. But Des is right, we don't have many rules with the kids but one of the major ones is no one in the house when we are at work, unless we know about it. Yeah, Jagger had Griffin here to help him study but he told us about it. And Griffin is Cadence's little brother, so he is our extended family. I look to Des to see him watching me so I just nod. We will figure out what will be best regarding Jagger.

As I yawn, feeling like this has been a day with forty-eight hours in it. Des gets up and goes to the head of the bed, reaches under my pillows, and grabs my pajamas. He tosses them my way as he pulls the covers down.

"Sugar, go on and get ready for bed. I'll make sure the house is locked down for the night. Meet ya back in bed shortly."

So tired I don't even argue with him. I do as he says and head to the bathroom to take off my makeup, wash my face, and brush my teeth. God, got to say so happy this day has finally come to an end.

Now we know kind of what we are going to have to address with Daisy. I don't know the next steps but between our family and the Horde I'm confident we will figure it out. And I'm thinking that the school needs to know what has been going on there. The bullying will definitely stop now if I have anything to say about it.

CHAPTER TWENTY-FOUR

DAISY

Lying in bed late morning, I'm trying to wrap my brain around yesterday. After the 'Docs' took care of my infected legs with draining and flushing the really bad ones, which hurt like hell, everyone visited a while then they all left.

We started to talk again but nothing heavy. Or better yet I talked and Mom, Des, and Jag listened. Watching my family during my ramblings I came to the realization that for some reason I was a total idiot, because I had their support and love. I truly had it. Somehow it got away from me. When I finally finished, Mom helped me to my bedroom so I could try and sleep. She never said one word about all the crap I laid at her feet. I shared a ton and the pain and anguish showed on her face. I don't ever want her to think any of this is her fault, because it's not. Somehow my brain waves got frazzled and I went out solo, trying to deal with crap I had no idea how to so I improvised. Again, I tried to reassure her that none of this has to do with her as my mom. It helped that Des shared some stories about when he was a kid and growing up. The struggles he experienced after his parents were killed and how he suffered with psychological issues due to having to step up to the plate—his words—and become the adult figure to his sisters and brother, while being a young adult himself. I think he put himself out there more for Mom than me so she could get how crap happens and it's no one's fault. Then Cadence and Trinity shared a bit, and man, didn't know how bad they both had it as kids. I felt so sorry for them both and thankful they found each other.

After Mom said good night and left, I stretched then laid back down in bed and for the first time in forever felt safe and secure. There was nothing at all to hide anymore from my family and the weight on my shoulders that has been lifted feels amazing. I can breathe even knowing that the work ahead of me is going to be very hard and overwhelming at times, but taking this first step—sharing my issues and secrets—helps me to realize that all the crap doesn't control me unless I let it. Also learned because of my family that it isn't weakness when you fall down. Only time it is, is when you refuse to get back up and fight.

I must have dropped off because the next thing I know someone is knocking on my door, waking me up. Before I can clear my throat, the door opens to Jag sticking his head in, trying to see if I'm awake or not. Shaking my head to clear it, I give my brother a small tentative smile, which he takes as an invitation to enter my room. He walks directly to me, watching me closely. Guess going to have to get used to the additional and intense watching that they will be doing. Brought that on myself and might be good for me to finally understand and accept that my thoughts and real life are two different things. Hearing Jag clear his throat, I realize that I drifted yet again. Raising just my head I give him big eyes. He just smiles like the goof he is.

"Hey, little Brat, how ya doin'? Wanted to check on you. Also you got a visitor, if you're up to it. Or just say the word and I'll get rid of 'em."

Struggling to clear my head, I'm wondering who would be here without a text or call. Doubt it's one of my queens because they're a lot like me and whenever we can grab some sleep, we are going to do that. Before I can ask Jag who, I see a shit-eating grin on his face as he tries to fill me in without laughing.

"Don't panic, Sis, but Griffin is here. Well, actually I saw him in his car on the street just watching the time about an hour ago. Finally got sick of waitin' for his ass to get out and come up to the door, so went out there and pulled him in. Feel up to company or want me to get rid of him?"

I literally leap out of bed and plow into Jagger, pushing him out of the way and run into our shared bathroom. Not even sure why he's back here again, but

I'm glad and even a little excited. Something about Griffin Powers feels like we are kindred souls. He doesn't seem to judge and as I've thought before, he is so cute.

By the time I'm dressed and heading down to the family room, I can hear my entire family talking over each other. Crap, it's going to be a shitshow for sure. I haven't had many boys, well actually, no boys come to see me. Des might be cleaning his gun while Mom tries to feed Griff, and I'm sure Jag is just sitting back and enjoying the show. As much as I love them all, wish they would find something to do. But then they wouldn't leave us alone, especially after the huge discovery of Jag's indiscretions with Sabrina over the summer.

Entering the room, I come to an abrupt stop. Des, Jag, and Griff are sitting around the fireplace talking quietly while Mom is serving up drinks yet again. Before I say anything 'he' sees me and jumps up, almost plowing in to Mom. She jerks back and loses her balance, falling right on Des's lap, who grabs her, holding her close, laughing. Everyone stops for a minute and stares. Mom is trying unsuccessfully to get up while Des continues to hold her close.

"Thanks, my man, for the gift of a beautiful woman in my lap. I owe ya. Hey, Daisy, look who's here for ya."

I approach the circus in my family room as Griff turns and reaches for the floor by the sofa, pulling up a bunch of flowers. Holy shit. Really, he brought those for me. And I see them coming when I realize what they are. Tie-dyed daisies. And a ton of them.

"Ummm, Daisy, I know yesterday was really hard and you're havin' a rough go of it, so thought I would come on by this morning to check on you and bring ya something to brighten your day. Well, that is what Trinity told me to do. Shit, I mean crap, wasn't supposed to tell ya that part, I guess."

I snort, trying not to laugh at how nervous he seems. Gosh, didn't think he of all the guys would be uncomfortable around girls. He always seems so put together, but giving it some thought, he also is generally by himself. Until he started to come around for Jagger's help, he kinda blended into school without a real crew or friends. He knew people but never saw him hanging with anyone in particular. Well, except that just about every girl who finds him drop-dead gorgeous is trying to hang off of him. Griff is generally quiet, a loner, as I said a gorgeous and a damaged soul. I've heard the murmurs between Mom, Trinity, Willow, and Archie. The stories about how the Powers boys grew up and what happened to them, not in great details but a high overview. And knowing that little bit my heart broke for them. Cadence seems to have gotten his stuff together when Trinity came into his life, though he has many issues still, as he said last night. That's where counseling has come into play for both of them. Lost in my thoughts, I hear a couple of throats clear and look up confused. Poor Griff is standing there, flowers pushed in my direction. Actually, his hand is trembling a bit while holding them my way. What a goof I am.

"Thanks, Griff, they are beautiful. Yeah, lots has been going on here. Yesterday was really hard but it needed to happen. Oh God, has anyone heard anything on Mary or Agnes? I'm such a horrible friend, haven't checked on either at all."

"Yeah, spoke to Akiria earlier, Brat, and she told me Mary is better and Agnes is hanging on. Both had setbacks yesterday, whatever the hell that means, but they are hanging on. Gonna be a long road for them both 'cause of fuckin' Sabrina and her crew of witches, but it's lookin' like, with lots of help, at least Mary will recover. Too soon for Agnes right now to know either way."

"Jag, watch your mouth, bub, before your mom's head starts spinnin' and she is spewin' green for Christ's sake, my man."

Mom's head twitches before she even turns to Des, giving him her big eyes with attitude. They go into a staredown and for once Mom wins, as he turns his head with a huge grin on his face. The guys both try not to laugh while I snort. Then we all bust out cackling. I reach over and grab the flowers, throwing over my shoulder to the room.

"Going to put these flowers in some water, be right back."

DAISY'S DARKNESS 179

As I head to the kitchen, I look out the window by the sink and see the sun shining and it feels so great to just be. Haven't felt like this in years. For this snapshot in time, I'm feeling good. Fingers crossed it can continue and grow each day. All I can wish for.

CHAPTER TWENTY-FIVE

GRIFFIN

Watching Daisy walkin' away with my flowers in her hands, I shift trying to keep her in my sight. That is until someone cracks me upside my head.

"All right, dude, knock it off, Griffin, that's my sister for God's sake. Do I need to ask you what your intentions are regarding her?"

Before I can even see if he is serious, I hear both Des and Dee Dee cracking up. Well, at least it isn't just me thinking Jagger is nuts.

I go grab a cup of coffee and sit my ass back down. No one says a word for a bit then Des breaks the uncomfortable silence. I keep tryin' to get a glimpse of Daisy, but no luck. She seemed to really like the flowers so gonna have to thank Trinity for the advice. Man, is my brother lucky to have a woman like her.

Sittin' here I'm trying to find a way to either get Daisy alone or figure out how to share some of my past without looking like a wimp. Over the years not many folks have had a clue what happened to us. Our father was a dick, no other way to describe him. Abusive doesn't even cover what he did. Cadence had it worse but the rest of us didn't have a walk in the park for sure.

So lost in my own thoughts, my hand holding the cup of coffee moves as someone drops onto the couch. I turn to see Daisy next to me and I smile at her. Then I put my coffee on the table and lean back, waiting to see where she's gonna go. Chicks scare me more than just about anything else in my life. But something about Daisy has tweaked my interest in more ways than one.

"Griff, it was really nice of you to get up early and bring those gorgeous flowers here. Thanks so much. Um, do you have plans for today?"

I shake my head 'cause as they say, cat's got my tongue. God, I would love to ask her to go out with me, maybe a drive or go to the zoo. Anything to spend some time together without parental eyes watching our every move.

We sit next to each other saying not a word. As minutes go by the silence is staggering. Not having a clue, I peek to my side to see Daisy looking right at me. She seems to be waiting. God, what is she expecting? This is why I don't do this stuff with girls. Or girls who are nothing like Heather, ya know, nice ones. So confusing. I feel a headache coming on. Great.

Des and Dee Dee are talking quietly before he looks at the two of us. Dee Dee squeezes his thigh, not saying a word.

"All right, Sugar, give me a minute for Christ's sake. Griff, if ya don't have anything going on, why don't you kids go do something? Catch a movie—go bowling—hit the zoo. Looks to be a good day, should make the most out of it. Right, Dee Dee?"

Grinning he waits for her to reply. I see her jam her elbow into his side. They're a riot. I wait patiently to see if Daisy's going to take Des's suggestion. At first she avoids looking my way, then finally glances at me, one eyebrow up. Damn, is she giving me attitude? Holy shit, she's gonna be a handful for sure. Can't wait, rather see her like this than beaten down.

"Griff, I'm not feeling like getting dressed up, you want to maybe hang here? We can watch a movie or maybe play some board games, if you like."

Yeah, I almost raise my fist up high I'm so excited, but catch myself at the last minute. Really cool, dipshit. I try to control my breathing, realizing the room is weirdly quiet with a strange vibe. Raising my head, I see them all staring at me. What? Did I miss something? Oh shit, Daisy asked me if I wanted to stay for a while. Can you say dumbass?

"Well, if ya don't mind, Daisy, would love to hang out today. I'm pretty easy so you can pick what you would rather do. Oh, and thanks for the invite."

She just nods looking to her mom, who is grinning widely. Well, Dee Dee looks happy which is good after yesterday. As we try to figure out what to do today, I just sit here lettin' it sink in. Without my brother, Cadence, having my back all those years ago, only God knows where I would be or even if I would still be breathing. And thanks to him, 'cause he brought the Horde into my life or brought me into theirs, however you look at it.

CHAPTER TWENTY-SIX

DAISY

I can't believe that Griff has spent the day with my family. We are pretty boring to say the least, but he seems to be soaking it all in. I mean everyone is home, plus our dog, Levi, and the two cats, Vinnie and China. *Full house as Des always says*, I think with a small smile on my face.

First, Mom made a late breakfast. As we sat around the table talking, it was pretty comfortable. Nothing heavy, which is good after last night. And all I revealed yesterday seemed to penetrate because she made me one poached egg with some fruit. Nothing else and no pressure, which I so appreciated. Now Des, Jag, and Griff stuffed their faces with eggs, bacon, potatoes, toast, and fruit. And lastly Mom made herself some scrambled eggs.

We all helped clean up then my family disappeared. I mean truly, one minute they were there, the next vanished. Turning to Griff I am lost for words.

He grins and moves to the sofa where he sits at the one side I usually end up at. Before I can think of anything to say, he motions for me to sit next to him.

"Daisy, after yesterday and how brave you were, I thought I'd share a couple of things with ya about my past. It ain't pretty, that's for sure, but it is what it is. Cadence always tells me, 'You are who you are and fuck anyone who has a problem with that.' But you were strong during a very emotional moment in time. I'm proud of ya, Lil' Flower. Now seeing how the Horde works, gotta figure ya'll have spoken about Cadence and his family. I mean, come on, Mom and I didn't get here until he'd been here awhile and freaked the hell out. Well, got to go back in history so you understand, we both had our own come to Jesus moment. Well, Cadence more than me, and that's due to him being older, and never tell him what I'm about to say, but smarter too. Our mom tended to pick the wrong men to settle down with. First our dad, who left us when I was like two or so. Then after a while she tried to get out there and date but can't imagine it was easy being a woman with three boys. Anyway, one guy started hanging out with us more and more. He was an asshole and jerk with us but not with Mom. Then one day she comes home telling my brothers and me that Duke and her were getting married, and he would be our new daddy. None of us boys were happy, especially Ryker for some reason. To keep this story movin', they got hitched and he moved in with us. Soon after our mom changed. Gone was the affectionate woman who loved her kids. She was always having 'accidents' like falling up or down stairs, walking into doors, and tripping on stuff we left on the floor. Well, if I remember correctly, one day she passed out in the backyard. The neighbor called an ambulance and she ended up in the hospital. Duke was now in charge of us and man did he turn into a bigger dick. At first we tried to put up a fight, but he showed his true colors. Now not gonna go into a lot of details but the Powers boys understand abuse. And that covers all kinds, just sayin'.

"It took my family a long time to get him out of our lives, but Mom finally did. We kind of all went our own way. Ryker joined the military. Cadence, well he used hookups to hide his pain. And I have tried to be the good boy for my mom. She struggled for years with her kids being all over. Being the youngest, I was with her but for a long time she had no idea where Ryker and Cadence were. When we moved here, it was for us to be close to my older brother and the family he found. He wasn't trying to erase us but find that missing piece in his damaged soul. Well, he found it all right in Trinity, and their story would break your heart. Not to mention our stepdad, Duke, is involved with some other lunatic. Had to do with, I think, human trafficking. Anyhow not trying to bring our relaxed moods down, but givin' you an idea that no matter what you're dealing with, if you put in the time and work you can eventually move the hell on. I still have issues and shit that comes up, but therapy over the years has literally kept me alive in my darkest hours. So yeah, I get Mary and Agnes 'cause been there, done that."

My mouth falls open with what just came out of his mouth. Someone like him had been to some counseling and even thought of suicide? No way, I've always thought of both for losers. God, what an idiot I am. Using my pain from Sabrina and the bullying, only thing I managed to do is bring more hurt on myself. Should have reached out, maybe I could have saved both Mary and Agnes the emotional distress they both have to be in. They pop in my head, still have no idea what's going on. Reaching over I hesitantly grab Griff's hand to get his attention.

"Hey, I'm so sorry you have gone through all of that Griff. If you ever need a shoulder I'm always here for you. I'm a firm believer that things happen for a reason and maybe you were brought to all of us when we both needed it. Oh, Griff, by the way, have you heard anything on either Mary or Agnes? Jag woke me when you got here so haven't been on social media and nothing from the queens either. They have been on my mind all night long."

Thinking that last sentence my eyes fill with tears. Again, such a wimp. Doing my ugly crying in front of the one guy who I not only like but who is hot; it's got to be very attractive, snot and tears all over my face. NOT. Probably going to scare him away with all of my emotional baggage and drama.

"No, haven't heard a word and was on Facebook

earlier. Don't they say no news is good news, Daisy? Gotta have faith and hope everything turns out right. There's nothing we can do for either of them right now. One thing I was running through my head is if Sabrina and that bunch of mean chicks have any idea how their constant razing and bullying pushed both girls to do what they did. I told my mom last night, and she couldn't believe, in today's world, that shit was still goin' on by other kids, especially girls doing it to other girls. I had to explain that some girls are worse than guys are. Anyway, maybe we will hear something soon. Fingers crossed, right?"

He looks my way briefly, then flips his eyes forward. That's strange. His face looks like he is trying not to laugh.

"Griff, anything wrong? What's funny? Come on, you can share with me."

Again he briefly glances my way and this time he can't hold back a smile that he quickly hides.

"What is it?"

Right before he answers me, Jag starts to walk in and when he sees me, stops and stares while his mouth drops open. Then he bursts into laughter holding his belly. Mom walks in behind him and when she manages to get by his dumb self, bent over cracking up, her head tilts to the side when we come into view. For a minute Mom doesn't say a word just looks between Griff and me. Then she moves toward us, never taking her eyes off of me. When I'm within reach, she grabs my hand and pulls me from the couch. Shocked, I follow her. As we make our way to the bathroom quietly, I hear from her whispers.

"You like him, don't you, Daisy? With everything going on yesterday we didn't get a chance to talk, just you and me. Well, remember if you are planning on spending time with a boy you want to impress, always use waterproof mascara, honey. Right now, you look like a drowned raccoon, just saying. Get in there and clean your face up while I handle your comedian brother. Glad he finds it so funny. If Griffin didn't say anything to you that's because he's a gentleman. And that's a good thing. So go on, wash your face and freshen up. I got some snacks in the oven and popcorn in the microwave. And hey, look at me, sweetie, the popcorn is light butter and I also have a veggie tray I threw together. I promised that I wasn't going to force you to eat and I won't. But I will offer you options. Deal?"

Looking at her, I feel it coming again and can't believe it. What is wrong with me, why am I so emotional? Great, waterworks part two. When Mom sees it, she pulls me in tightly and holds me close while I let my inner wuss out. And it feels good.

CHAPTER TWENTY-SEVEN

DEE DEE

The rest of the weekend goes by with no major problems. Joe let us know that Mary was being moved to the observation floor. He also told us there was no change at all in Agnes. God, don't want to tell Daisy but she has been on me, so finally gave her the news. Her face paled as she wrapped her arms around her middle. Then she asked to be excused and headed to her bedroom.

I'm going through some bills when Des, Cadence, and Wolf walk through the back door. All seem to be extremely pissed off for some unknown reason. And this in itself is strange to see the three of them mad at the same time. The trio is hardly ever unbalanced. If one or two are struggling or upset, the last man tries to be the voice of reason. So, I'm curious to see what they have been up to.

All three drop down in chairs around the table, elbows bent, leaning forward, all eyes on me. Wolf looks around then back at me, his eyes filled with worry.

"Dee Dee, how's Daisy doing today? Des said she's hanging in, which is a good thing. Glad to hear she is planning on going to therapy on Monday. Gabriel also shared he is gonna talk to some folks who specialize in her specific issues. The road ahead is gonna be rough but she can do it. I have faith in her."

He stops abruptly, looking to Des and I see my man barely nod in his direction. If I wasn't watching I would have missed it. Taking a minute, I look at each man, noticing their visible unease in the way they are holding their bodies, as if one thing could set them off into a rage. Holy cow, what now? Before they can get it together enough, I jump the gun.

"Okay, let me have it. What's wrong? And don't tell me nothing because y'all are wound up tighter than a banjo string. Des, what's up? You don't usually have a problem speaking your mind...so speak."

"Damn it, woman, all right. Calm yourself, will ya, and keep it down, don't want to upset Daisy. Got nothin' to share that's why we're pissed. Jag told us where Sabrina lived so we drove over, sat outside, and waited. After about forty-five minutes with nothing we moved on. Every stop was a waste of our time. Finally drove past the hospital and I ran up to see if Joe or Melody were there. And of course they were, along with George and his wife, Betty. They were beyond exhausted and I'm guessin' the adult kids around them were Agnes's older siblings. I checked in with them briefly and Joe walked me back down. I asked about Agnes and he just shook his head. Apparently, the longer she is unconscious and doesn't wake up, the worse the prognosis is. Doctors are saying it's a waiting game right now. And if she does wake up, they have no idea what shape she will be in or if there will be brain damage, the severity of it, on top of all the other bullshit goin' on. It's a fuckin' shitshow."

Reaching over I grab his hand, giving it a squeeze. He just stares at our hands then his eyes move to my face. I can tell everything going on is weighing heavily on him. When we got together he accepted both kids as his own. Never has he shown in any of his actions that Jagger and Daisy aren't his kids. He would fight to the death for them, I'm sure. And being the alpha that he is, not having control of a situation is killing him.

"All right, so we are at a standstill. Nothing we can do but keep putting one foot in front of the other, guys. Until something breaks, or we get news on either girl, we have to try and live our lives as normal as possible. Daisy needs that more than anything right now. Don't you agree?"

The guys kind of shake their heads, but no one says a word. We sit at the table, everyone in their own world, when Jagger enters the kitchen, looks around, and shakes his head. He grabs a flavored water and sits next to Wolf.

"So what's goin' on? What's with the long faces? Just checked on Brat, she's curled up asleep."

Cadence gives him a head nod, looking at his water,

so as usual I get up and grab a couple of bottles, putting them in the middle of the table. Before I can sit, they are gone. God, cat got their tongues? All they have to do is ask, or better yet, help themselves for Christ's sake. Been over this a hundred times. Cadence takes a long drink, setting the bottle down, giving Jagger all his attention.

"Bro, I had a chat this morning with Griffin. He mentioned that when Daisy was tormented by Sabrina, a boy's name came up. Ya know a Joey? Have any idea who this prick is? 'Cause from what Griffin shared, this asshole not only put his hands on our girl but caused her needless pain. So I'm thinkin' we need to find this son of a bitch, and not only kick his ass but beat it out of him—if needed—to find out what or who was involved besides that bitch Sabrina."

He raises an eyebrow at my son, impatiently waiting for an answer. Jagger's hands clench and his eyes glare at our friend, fury and anger in them. "Really, dude, you think if I knew who he was his ass wouldn't already be hurtin'? I've racked my brain and got no idea of any Joey. When Sabrina and I were together, didn't do a lot of talkin' or sharin' of the crowds we hung with."

Cadence smirks and as usual runs his mouth before thinking.

"Yeah, heard all about what ya were doin' and know talkin' wasn't high on the list. Does she have any relatives with the name Joe that you know of?"

Watching the two marking their territory I'm

getting frustrated. Now is not the time to be pissing in the sandbox. We need to pull together and try to support Daisy at her time of need. Before I can preach to these adolescents, Jagger stands up, knocking his chair backward and it falls to the ground.

"Holy shit, Cadence, you hit it on the head for Christ's sake. I was at a family picnic with the bitch, sorry, Mom. A lot of her family was there, and yeah, she has a cousin older than us named Joe. That's probably who she dragged in for help. From what her family was saying, he's a loser, dropped out of school, has a drug problem and a record already. Des, you and Mom made a police report, should we let them know that the 'Joey' is probably Sabrina's older cousin? Think it would help?"

As we sit around the table, they are renewed with this new information. Personally, I don't care if they catch who was there that day. I'm more concerned about my daughter, her state of mind, and her two friends fighting for their lives. I get up and walk down the hall to check on her. Quietly opening the door, I hear her sniff so I move as fast as I can to the side of her bed, reaching and pulling her into my arms.

"Daisy, honey what's wrong? Bad dream? Come on, tell me, I can't help you without knowing what you're dealing with. Please. Honey, let me help you."

Shaking her head, she wipes her nose with her arm then lifts her head, eyes wet and red.

"Mom, I woke up and for some reason felt down. Probably from all my emotions from yesterday. And the first thing to pop into my head is going in the bathroom and cutting myself to relieve the darkness and pain. Why, oh God, why is this happening? What if I can't stop or there is something mentally wrong with me, Mom? Please promise not to put me in a crazy ward. I can't even think, I don't want to be put in a hospital. That would kill me. I want to get better and know I need help. Don't know if even with help I'll be able to stop the constant darkness and sadness in my soul. Why am I like this? Jagger's fine, well you know what I mean, he is crazy but his own bat-ass crazy. How come I'm cursed with the lunatic gene?"

Exhausted, she falls back into my arms bawling. I hold her close, knowing this is part of the healing process. She's got a long road ahead of her and, yeah, I'm sure a few bumps in the road. She doesn't know yet her own strength but we'll get her there. There is no other option. Love her too much.

As we sit together on her bed, holding each other, I begin to understand how very lucky I am. My daughter is right here, we have the chance to move forward and work this crap out. My mind goes to the two girls in the hospital right now, and I can't even comprehend how their folks must feel. Tears fill my eyes as I thank God for his blessings keeping our girl with us.

CHAPTER TWENTY-EIGHT

DAISY

I'm exhausted even with an entire weekend of just resting and recouping. Well, I got more sleep these last two days than in the past three to six months. I feel rested on one hand and weak on the other. Last night, I told my family to quit walking on eggshells around me, it's driving me crazy. Well, that opened the door for my big brother to return to the goof he always is. Couldn't take another minute of him being so serious. Des and Mom are being so careful with me too. Even though I totally appreciate it, want to go back to our everyday routines. Nope, that's not true. Further back, when all my craziness started. Before the binging—purging—self-hurting—cutting. The times when we had fun together without all the emotional baggage that has dropped into our lives.

"Lil' Brat to earth, come in, Daisy, you there?"

Hearing Jag's voice I turn his way. We're in his car on the way to school. Wish I could have gotten out of another day, but Mom said I need to try and keep my life going forward. As usual she's right, won't tell her that.

"Yeah, I'm here. What's up?"

"Daisy, I asked ya if you're all right? I figure this is gonna be hard but remember always, sister of mine, that it's us against the world. Right?"

Kind of giggling I just nod. Yeah, a total goof. But without him, don't know where I would be headed. He took the time to figure me out and had the guts to tell Mom and Des. Without his help, not sure how much longer I would have been able to hang on.

As we get closer to school, I start to feel my anxiety rising. Oh God, please let me do this. Spoke to my queens this weekend and shared some of the crap going on. They as usual have my back which I already knew in my heart. The girls also communicated some of their own personal struggles too. Can't believe how much we've drifted apart. Got to pay attention and not let that ever happen again.

Jag finds a parking space and we get out of the car, heading toward school. I see Bird, Akiria, Amethyst, and V as they run/skip toward me. I'm surrounded by them, trying to take in everything they are saying, which is impossible because they are all talking at the same time. I just soak up the feeling of their friendship until I hear a loud whistle. I look around and see Jag pulling two fingers out of his mouth.

"All right, ladies, let's get a move on it. Ya don't want to be late now, do you?"

We laugh as we move toward our high school. As we head to our lockers, I see Jag pull Akiria back. Don't even want to think what that's all about. Looking back up, I see Bird, V, and Amethyst turning back to me with big eyes. I glance past them to see Griff leaning against my locker, waiting for me. I get all warm just seeing him. All weekend, besides the day he was over, he's been texting me, checking in on me. Don't think he knows how much it means to me.

Come to think about it, the whole Horde has been making sure I'm all right. Fern stopped by with a huge veggie tray for me. She's so awesome because I know Mom shared my eating problems. Willow and Archie came by with some flowers and balloons to cheer me up. Hope, Trinity, and Cadence stopped in the same day Griff was over. Hope tried her best to draw me a picture of her and me. That made me cry because across the top was written, 'I love my best friend Daisy.' Looking at it, I realize she didn't write it but still the same I will treasure it forever. It's hanging on my bulletin board in my room. Wolf brought me a beautiful leather-bound journal to write my thoughts in. And he smudged my room, telling me it helps cleanse a space and invites positive energy into it. I want to learn more of that kind of stuff and told him that. The smile on his face showed how happy he was to hear that.

"Hey, Lil' Flower, ya okay? Know how hard this is so thought I'd walk ya to class."

As everyone stands around, for the first time I see

how lucky I am to have each of them in my life. I'm not alone and it's not just my family. Spending a few minutes catching up, talking about nothing in general, we hear the loudspeaker squeak, which is a sign someone is about to speak. Our principal says good morning and then tells us that there is a special assembly in ten minutes. All students should plan on attending so it was being held in the football stadium. When he finishes, we all look at each other. Jag, of course, speaks first.

"Wonder what bullshit is comin' our way. Let's head over so we can all sit together at least."

So in a group with Jag and Akiria first, followed by Bird, Amethyst, and V and finally Griff and I bringing up the rear, we start the trek to the stadium. I'm curious about what's going on, well until my hand is held and Griff moves a bit closer to me. Then all I can think about is walking next to him holding hands.

We make it to the stadium and find enough seats to sit together. Everyone plants their butts down. Somehow Griff is on my left, Jag is on my right. The whole place is loud and I feel a slight headache coming on. When I look up and see Principal Phillips walking across the stage, I suddenly feel like something really bad is about to happen. My body starts trembling. Griff looks at me, leaning down, asking me if I'm okay. I just nod because I can't find my voice. Jag grabs my other hand while we all sit and wait for the assembly to start. When our principal taps the microphone, the place starts to quiet down. She patiently stands at the podium until you can hear a pin drop.

"Good morning. I apologize for the short notice but what I'm about to say is extremely important so please bear with me. The first item that has been brought to my attention is from two students' parents. They told me their children have been the victims of severe bullying in this school. This is unacceptable."

My head jerks up at this. Oh God. Could she know about all the crap Mary and Agnes have been through? Jag said there was very little on social media about their attempts that he could see, and Griff said no one he knows said a word. Feeling my heart start to pound, our principal continues on.

"Now, before you get out of hand, please give me a moment. As of today, there will be additional school patrols throughout the grounds. We have two rooms that will be open throughout the day to report if you become of victim of bullying. No one not in attendance of this school is allowed without a pass from the office. Please be aware of surroundings. The patrols will be keeping a close eye in the hallways of our school also."

She takes a moment grabbing a water, taking a couple of sips before placing it back down. *She looks either nervous or upset*, I think to myself.

"The next item is something no principal ever wants to happen within her school. It is with a very heavy heart that I share this very sad news. Earlier this morning, I received a call from Agnes Newton's parents. They wanted me to know what had transpired over the weekend. I'm sure some of you are aware that Agnes made an attempt to commit suicide and her mother found her. She has been in the hospital since Friday in the Intensive Care Unit. Mr. Newton informed me that at 5:13 a.m. this morning, Agnes passed away peacefully surrounded by her family."

Hearing a keening noise coming from somewhere my head starts to pound. I'm having a hard time trying to catch my breath. The whole place is in shock, but that noise is so full of pain you can almost physically feel it. Who or what is that, for God's sake? Before I can stand and look around, I'm pulled to my feet.

"Daisy, Sis, calm the fuck down. Come on, breathe in and out. Try to take in some air before you pass out. Sis, listen to my voice. Close your eyes and just hear my voice. Daisy, it's Jagger your pain in the ass brother. Take in slow breaths, that's it, in through your noise out through your mouth. Hold on to me, Daisy, I gotcha. I gotcha. Griffin, call the garage tell my mom and Des to get their asses here. NOW!"

Not sure what is going on but my head is throbbing uncontrollably. I feel something drip down my face from my nose, so I go to wipe it. Looking down, my hand is covered in blood. What? Oh my God, I have a bloody nose.

"Jag, my nose is bleeding for some reason. I need to go to the bathroom."

Bird and Akiria both reach for some tissues. Jag looks down, shaking his head.

"I have to go, Jag, your shirt is getting blood on it. Look at my hands. Please let me go."

As I try to get away he refuses to release me. I start to really fight him but he's too strong and I don't have much fight in me. Feeling someone behind me, I assume it's Griff.

"Assholes, let me GOOOOOOOOOO! Oh God no...no...no. Not Agnes. Why? Oh God, why? How could this have happened, she's just a kid? Let me go, Jag. Oh God, noooooo. LET ME GO! LET ME GO! I can't, no, not now, she was in the hospital, how could she die? They were supposed to save her."

Immediately I'm surrounded by the queens. Looking around every one of them is shocked with tears running down their faces. Bird reaches over, grabbing my hand, squeezing tightly. Akiria is running her hand up my other arm, while V tries to get as close as possible to my side. Amethyst stands to the side looking stunned. My eyes meet hers and she falls, shatters right in front of me, hitting the ground hard. Akiria goes to her, pulling her into her arms, rocking back and forth. The thundering in the assembly is deafening. My ears actually are ringing. Feeling nauseated, I try again to get away but the more I try, the harder Jag holds me to him. Griff is gently running his hands up and down my back, occasionally massaging my shoulders. Any other time this would feel beyond wonderful. Right now it makes my skin crawl and I want to scream.

As the principal tries to get control of the assembly, my legs feel like they can't hold me up much longer. I'm not going to be able to handle the news of Agnes's death. No, her suicide. She killed herself. My newest friend is dead because of the bullying by Sabrina and her mean girl clique. *I'm going to kill her with my bare hands*, I think to myself. All at once I feel warm and dizzy. Again, I can't breathe or even talk. I feel it right before it happens. The darkness starts to take over as my body lets go. The last thing I hear are two voices screaming... "DAISY!"

Penetrating the black hole I've fallen into is a constant beeping. I wish it would just stop. Not sure what is going on, but one thing I know is that I prefer the dark murkiness where I'm at than trying to wake up into my life. I don't remember much, but grasp that something is lurking in the back of my mind. Something really bad. When I try to recall it, I go blank. I'm so very tired and as the weight of gloom presses down on me, I give in and fall back into a troubled sleep.

CHAPTER TWENTY-NINE

DEE DEE

Watching Daisy sleep, my mind is empty and void. How can this be happening? My daughter has been dealing with so much, when does it stop? She needs a break for damn sure. The only thing I can do is hold her hand and pray. By the time we were able to get to the school, find the stadium, and spot the kids, she was passed out and suffering with a horrible bloody nose. When we couldn't get her to wake up, Des called 911.

Her brother, Griffin, and girlfriends were also in shock. Jag wouldn't let go of his sister until the paramedics actually pulled him away, with the help of Des. As they loaded her up on a stretcher, Jag broke down and lost it. Des grabbed him close saying nothing. My heart hurt just looking around seeing all the kids suffering in one way or another. I hear a noise from the front.

"Attention please, your attention. We have counselors on hand in the office next to Human

Resources to help you process this devastating news. Please remember there is no weakness in admitting you need help. My door also is always open, and every teacher and the office staff are here to help. We will get through this together. And please keep Agnes and her family in your thoughts and prayers at this very difficult time."

My head jolts at her last words. What? Why do they need to keep them in their prayers? My eyes look to Jagger, who is already looking my way. I'm afraid to ask but need to know. I mouth, 'Did Agnes die?' He closes his eyes and nods his head. My heart immediately breaks for George, Betty, and their family. Oh what a waste of a promising young girl's life.

The paramedics have Daisy loaded up and are moving out. We go to follow them out when I hear Jagger telling everyone to stay in school, he'll let them know how his sister is doing. Knowing what is coming next, I hear Griffin's voice tell Jagger he will drive him to the hospital. Before my son can argue, I hear his friend tell him he's in no shape to be behind the wheel of a car. Trying to keep up, I start to lose it when an arm comes around me, pulling me close. As usual, Des is at my side when I need him the most.

Once our daughter is loaded up, Des gives me a hand into the back of the ambulance, telling me he will meet me there. I just nod then turn, going to the bench the paramedic points to. After sitting and keeping an eye on what was being done to my daughter, I do the only thing I can think of. I ask the good Lord to protect my Daisy and bring her back to me whole.

A nurse enters the room telling me I need to step out, they need to run some tests on Daisy. I ask if I can go with and they tell me she is going for X-rays, an EKG, and an ultrasound. She will come find me when they are done.

After giving Daisy a kiss on her forehead, whispering I love her, I watch as they move her down the hall and turn left. Turning myself, I follow the signs, walking slowly to the waiting room. My head is going in every direction but I have no idea about what. Seeing a bathroom, I stop and relieve my full bladder. While washing my hands the feeling overtakes me. Tears start to build up and trickle down my cheeks. Feeling my emotions taking over, I sit back down on the toilet, holding my head, trying to catch my breath. Have to be strong, no matter what. The kids need me more than ever. After maybe five or ten minutes, I stand and go to the sink to clean off my face. Brushing my hair back and drying my hands, I head out the door and run right into something hard. Feeling arms around me, a familiar warmth surrounds me and I breathe in all that is Des. He always knows. How, don't know. Pulling me off to the side, he just holds me, saying not a word, and it's just what is needed. Aware of his strength, I soak it in to build me back up. After a while, lifting my head, my eyes glance up to see him already looking at me. Leaning down he lays a soft kiss on my lips. Then he turns us toward the waiting room.

When we enter, I instantly stop. The room has been taken over by Daisy's friends and the Horde. Looking around I'm wondering who is at the garage when Des whispers into my ear softly, "Closed the garage, honey. Family first, always."

Everyone in the room is watching when Fern and Trinity move toward us. Des steps away as the women pull me into their arms. Knowing that they are here for Daisy and to support us, again unable to fight it, I break down.

After greeting everyone I take a seat between Jagger and Des. The room is eerily silent as we wait for news. I can't believe we are in a hospital again, but this time it's for one of our own kids. My heart feels like it is breaking as time goes by with no word at all.

This is the hardest part...waiting.

CHAPTER THIRTY

DES

These hospital chairs suck, I think to myself, just as I feel Dee Dee relax against me, telling me she's finally crashed. I look around, seeing quite a few folks are either kind of dozing or totally sacked out. Not much else to do while we wait. Wolf catches my eye, motioning drinking, guessin' coffee. I nod then watch as he goes by Cadence giving him a bump. They both head to the door and leave. Jagger is on the other side of Dee Dee, head in his hands, which are leaning on his knees. His one leg is jumping all over the fuckin' place. Yeah, this shit isn't easy for Christ's sake.

I catch motion out of the corner of my eye as Trinity walk/waddles her way to Jagger. Falling into the chair, she pulls him into her, holding on tightly. He drops his head to her shoulder, and after a short time, I see his shoulders shaking. Trinity just runs her hands through his hair.

Feelin' someone sit next to me, I look to see Griffin

there. His face shows everything, and it dawns on me this kid seems to be sweet on Daisy. Knowin' his story, not sure I'm too thrilled with it either. He's a good kid, for sure, but also damaged with a ton of fuckin' baggage. And Daisy is fightin' her own demons, doesn't need to take on anyone else's. But on the other hand, when he's around I see the old Daisy come out. She smiles more, and somehow, he calms her down. Whatever...like I have any say so. These kids nowadays ain't gonna listen to their parents.

The door opens up and I'm guessin' some type of doctor enters.

"Daisy Sutton family?"

Moving Dee Dee, I gently wake her up. She's confused for a minute then looks around, stopping at the doctor. She leaps up, walking directly to him. I follow behind as everyone else surrounds us.

"Are you the family of Daisy Sutton?"

Dee Dee nods her head.

"All of you? Due to HIPPA, I can only speak to her family."

I explain to him that yes, we all are her family. He looks around before clearing his throat.

"All right, right now we are waiting on results from some additional tests performed on Daisy. Her blood pressure is moderately high, which might explain the bloody nose. Her white blood count is also elevated, which might indicate an infection somewhere. Noticed some cuts on her thighs and there is one slightly inflamed. We will talk about those in a bit. She hasn't woken up yet, which is most concerning. Did she hit her head when she passed out, was anyone with her?"

Jagger steps up and explains what happened. He tells the doctor she didn't hit her head, but she already had the bloody nose before passing out. Nodding at Jagger the doctor looks to Dee Dee and me.

"We are going to keep Daisy here for observation. Especially with finding out what she found out in school today about one of her friends. After my physical examination, I noticed that she has some signs of suffering from either bulimia or anorexia. Did you know this, and what is being done to help her? Also, the cuts and scars are indicating she is also a cutter. Please tell me she is in counseling? This can escalate quicker than you can imagine."

I hear Griffin tell everyone to give us some privacy. As they all go to take their seats, Dee Dee, Jagger, and I gather around the doctor. Dee Dee tells him what we recently found out regarding Daisy's conditions. He nods while making notes on an iPad.

"Good, now that you know what's been going on, maybe she can get the help she definitely needs. Hopefully, it's been caught soon enough not to cause permanent damage. Our plan is to keep your daughter on an observation floor for at least tonight, or until she wakes up. We will start an IV with saline solution and an antibiotic drip. Until she comes to, our hands are kind of tied. So you both know, the longer Daisy is unconscious there are risks and issues that can arise. If we get to that point, I'll make sure to have a conversation with you. Any questions?"

Nothing comes to mind, so he lets us know once they have a room someone will let us know. I raise my hand to him. We shake and I thank him for taking care of Daisy. After he turns and exits, I lean into Dee Dee. Jagger gets closer. He asks if maybe we should send everyone home.

"Ain't gonna happen, boy. Someone will be here at all times, just their way. Maybe send the kids home, let them know if there is a change you'll let them know, send a text."

He acknowledges his agreement and moves to where all the teenagers are gathered. Turning to Dee Dee, I search her face. It's filled with worry, despair, and pain.

"She'll be okay, Dee Dee, let's not lose faith. Okay, Sugar?"

Feeling her nod, I pull her closer.

Waking up I try to shift to a more comfortable position, but Dee Dee's body is so close to mine, can't move. Fuck, my shoulder is killin' me and my arm is tingling like a son of a bitch 'cause it's asleep. Probably not the best idea to let my woman fall asleep on my arm for goddamn sake. Shifting my head, the first thing I see is Jagger asleep in the recliner. My eyes move to the hospital bed where Daisy is still unconscious. Thinking back to earlier, after she was moved to this room, well fuck, it's more like a hotel suite for Christ's sake. Thank God we have health insurance 'cause if we didn't, probably would have to sell an organ to pay the bill. And I would have done it without hesitating for one minute. Anything for my girl Daisy.

We were told we could come in for a couple of minutes and then will have to go home. They'll call if there are any changes. At the last comment, Dee Dee lost her shit. After I managed to get her under control again, I made my way to the nurses' station. There were three nurses at the desk, two very young and the last looked like she should have retired years ago. I started very nice and friendly and ended up threatening to sue, not only the hospital but each of them. There was no way in hell we were gonna leave our girl here alone. When she wakes up, she will see a face she knows. The head nurse was called and after much back-and-forth banter—explaining hospital policy—threats to call the cops and throwing us out; not to mention some bullshit I had no idea what she was even talking about. Throughout the whole debacle, I stood my ground and I guess she finally got that I wasn't gonna take any crap right now. And that's the story of how we managed to stay with Daisy.

Feeling Dee Dee stir and moving, I wait to see if she's actually waking up or just shifting. This has to be the most uncomfortable motherfucking couch ever. My body feels like it has been beaten up. Lying in the quiet, early morning hours, I reflect on the events of the last twenty-four hours. When we got the call from Griffin, not sure who was more worried Dee Dee or me. I drove to the school with my woman praying out loud as I blew through light after light. Seeing Daisy unconscious, being taken in an ambulance almost killed me. What the fuck, do we have a black cloud over our house? Or has someone placed one of those, what the hell are they called, 'wicca' spells-curses or whatever the fuck. It seems like once shit starts it just keeps piling up.

Raising her head, Dee Dee's sleepy eyes find mine and she gives me a small smile.

"Any change, Des?"

"Sugar, not yet. Hey, our girl is a fighter, we just gotta be patient. Come on, let's sit up. This fuckin' couch is killing me. Pure torture."

Hearing her lightly chuckle I smile to myself. Yeah, gotta keep my woman's frame of mind positive. We have a long road ahead of us.

CHAPTER THIRTY-ONE

GRIFFIN

Not being able to stay at the hospital just about killed me. Been texting Jagger until he told me get some sleep, if there is a change, he would let me know. Well, haven't been able to get any shut-eye, too much running through my head. What the ever-loving fuck? I can't believe Agnes is dead. How can it be, one day not too long ago we are rescuing her and now she is gone? Makes me so angry 'cause she seemed like such a good kid. This is gonna kill Daisy. She will blame herself even more because she ignored the texts when she was dealing with her own shit.

Getting out of bed, I head to the bathroom, take a piss, and jump in the shower. Mom's not up yet but will be soon. Figure might as well get an early start, can't keep missing school. And today I'm gonna try and find Sabrina, Heather, and any of other mean girl clique. I need to find out where Joey is. Making quick work of washing, I step out, dry off, and get dressed. I brush my teeth, run a comb through my hair, and done.

After going back to my room I make my bed. Yeah, if I don't, Mom has a hemorrhage so easier just to do it. Then I go to the kitchen, pushing the coffee button so it's ready when she gets up. I've been pretty absent lately and not doing my share to help her out. Moving to toss some shit in the garbage, I notice it's flowing over so I pull it and go dump it in the trash outside. Then I come back in and unload and reload the dishwasher. After I wipe down the counters, I then grab a bowl, spoon, a box of cereal, and a banana to cut up. I chow down, drinking some orange juice to wash down the Cinnamon Toast Crunch, one of my favorites.

Hearing footsteps, my head turns just as Mom walks in. Seeing me, she stops for a second or two then comes right to me, giving me a half-ass hug.

"How's she doing?"

I shake my head not saying a word.

"Did Des and Dee Dee spend the night?"

As we have a conversation about Daisy's situation, I finally tell Mom I don't know much since I left. She grabs coffee and must notice some of the shit I took care of this morning. Grinning and shaking her head, she again comes my way and ruffles my hair. "Thanks, Griffin, for taking care of that. Hope you know how much I appreciate your help around here. You're a good kid."

"Yeah, better than those other two you had. They are total asswipes. Just sayin', Mom."

She laughs while drinking her coffee and we come to a comfortable morning quiet. These are my favorite times 'cause I'm with my mom.

Looking at the time, know I gotta move my ass. I get up and give her a kiss. On my way to my bedroom to grab my shit I tell her if something changes with Daisy, I'll let her know.

"Bye, Mom, have a good day. Love ya."

"You too, sweetie. I love you more. And Griffin she will be okay, baby. I feel it here."

Then she points to the left side of her chest where her heart is.

As I head to school, my head is remembering when my shit hit the fan years ago and Mom found me a therapist. At first, I was so against it, but after the day I held Mom's pain pills in one hand and a razor blade in the other, I knew I was in desperate need of help. My abuse threw me off and I was held back in school for two years. Gave me time to process and try and get my crap together.

As I pull into the student parking lot, it seems pretty light. Bet a lot of the kids are staying home after that assembly yesterday. I ain't got that option, too much needs to be done. After parking, I walk to the school—kind of in my own mind—not paying attention. Before it happens, I feel something, not sure what, right when I'm surrounded by Daisy's girls. They are all talking at the same time and I can't understand a word.

"Hey, can't hear a word anyone is saying. You're

screeching it, killin' my ears so calm the hell down and try to talk, one at a time, for Christ's sake."

They look at each other shocked at what I said. Finally, after some discussion, Bird comes up to me. Quietly she asks if there is any news about Daisy. I explain about last night with Jagger and that I haven't gotten anything today. We stand in the hallway talking and remembering Agnes, who I didn't know that well. The girls want to know how Mary is doing, so I pass on the news that Dee Dee shared yesterday in the waiting room. The bell rings, warning us about first classes. I promise them to keep them informed if I hear anything.

We all move, heading to our classes, as another day starts.

Sitting in my psychology class I feel my phone vibrating, so I reach down grabbing it. When I see the name of who is calling my stomach drops. Jagger. As much as I wanted to call him all morning, I held back. Shit, better grab it, so I swipe the screen as I stand and quickly leave the class.

"Sorry, Jagger, had to leave my class. What's up, brother?"

"Hey, Griffin, just checkin' in. She's still out, no change. They are doing more tests today and another doctor stopped by and examined Daisy. She asked if she was involved in an accident or trauma, or has a lot of stress in her life. When Mom explained what's been going on, she said that sometimes our brain or body can't take anymore so it takes a break to give some healing time. She explained that Daisy has been experiencing, for a long period of time, a lot of emotional, physical, and psychological trauma. She did a couple of neurological tests and Daisy did respond, so she promised to stop in throughout the day and also was gonna speak to the other doctor. Guess it's not bad news, we knew she had too much shit constantly rolling around in her head. That she was able to even function is shockin', brother. That's all I got right now. Will keep ya in the loop. Keep an eye out for the bitch Sabrina, would ya?"

We speak for a couple of minutes then he hangs up to get back to his family. I take a couple of deep breaths then head back to class. It's going to be a very long day. I'm guessing no news is good news. I cross my fingers that's true.

CHAPTER THIRTY-TWO

DAISY

Feeling like I'm floating on clouds, my head feels extremely foggy. That dang beeping is what catches my attention again. I try to move and just feel like my body isn't listening. Taking a couple of breaths, I can feel something in my nose. Not sure where I'm at, but it's quiet, which is peaceful. I try to clear my brain. Why am I here, can't remember...oh my God, AGNES. It hits me hard and I wish for my brain to shut off, or that I could go back to that deep sleep. My heart hurts so bad for her. Wish it would have turned out differently, but sometimes bad things happen to good people, Mom always says.

I'm drifting in and out of consciousness when the beeping gets faster. Then I hear footsteps and a voice asking for a nurse. Who is that and why can't I open my eyes, they feel so heavy? Suddenly I can feel hands on me as someone tells others to get out for a minute. This is right before once again I drift back to La-la Land.

The next time my mind seems a bit clearer, but I still can't open my eyes or even move. I start to worry that maybe I did this to myself. Could have cut too deep, hit an artery and am in a coma? Or from the bingeing and purging could have ruptured something inside of me. The nightmare that Agnes died and we had an assembly in school might have been my imagination. I can't trust my thoughts and don't have the ability to ask anyone. Besides the beeping I now can hear murmuring, but can't make out the words or even who it is. As my mind lingers, trying to figure out this puzzle, the heaviness starts to take over and again I fade back into the abyss.

Now when my body tries to function I feel pain in my head, stomach, and legs where I've cut. The sounds in the room are much clearer, even though I have no idea how much time has passed. How long have I been like this? Are Mom and Des still here or have they given up on me? What about Jag? I know that I'm a disappointment with all my craziness. Why did this happen now when I finally outed myself and was even planning on going into intense therapy? I've wasted so much time, for what? To end up like this. I feel so down and blue right now. My heart feels heavy as I lie here, not knowing what's going on, but I can feel the tears rolling down my face, and someone gently wiping them away. The absolute desolation in my soul pulls me back under again toward the darkness.

Something, what is that? I feel someone, I think, holding my hand and whispering to me. Taking a few breaths, I try to open my eyes, and this time they not only open but I'm instantly blinded by the startling bright lights. Closing them immediately, I again open them after blinking a couple of times, this time slightly, so I can adjust my reflexes. When my vision finally is used to the brightness, I open my eyes and try to focus. I continue to peek around until finally my eyes adjust to being able to see. Laying here, eyes open, I work on moving my hand with the heavy weight on it. It's not painful but something tells me to just move at least a finger. So for a bit, I tell my brain to move something—anything. I beg and plead but can't seem to make anything happen. So again, I take a break. Glancing around I see the room is pretty big. There are medical machines around me and some kind of medicine going through a hose, probably into my arm. Feeling like trying again, I push myself. Concentrating on getting that hand to flex in my mind's eye, I imagine my hand moving, flexing, and reaching for what or whoever is right there. My hand is tingling and not sure but finally something happens, I just don't know what. Again and again, I force myself to move. Feeling exhausted, I take another break. Taking in a deep breath, I close my eyes and try to relax.

Suddenly I feel the pressure in my hand and realize that someone is actually holding and squeezing my hand. After the last squeeze, I put everything into it and softly my hand grasps back. I hear a noise then a chair being pushed back.

"Oh my God, I felt her hand grip mine. Des, Jagger,

I think she's coming round, get a nurse. Daisy, honey, it's Mom, come back to us. Fight as hard as you can, don't leave us. Please, honey, open those beautiful eyes for me."

Hearing the sadness as she speaks, once again, I fight the feeling to just go under toward the darkness and manage to get my eyes to open up and I see Mom right in front of me. She is watching me with such love on her face, I feel that deeply. Coming up behind her, Des comes into view, then Jag is looking over his shoulder. They all stare at me like a miracle just happened. Duh, guys, I opened my eyes.

"Umph, hey, morning, I guess."

They look at me then each other before such relief appears on each of their faces and I give them a very small smile. Then feeling extremely tired, I drift away again without another word.

For the next day or so I'm able to keep my eyes open longer each time. My CBC showed I have an infection, so antibiotics are ordered. Jag went back to school and Des to the garage, but no one could get Mom away from the side of my bed. Des stopped one night on his way here and picked up a thick sleeping bag so Mom could be a bit more comfortable on the couch from hell. No idea what that even means. I'm not eating much, on a very bland liquid diet right now. They are going to try to sit me up today at the side of the bed. And their on-staff crisis counselor is scheduled to come in and see me. I'm not going to argue at all.

After my sponge bath, I'm sitting up, and Mom grabs both hands, kissing my knuckles. Looking at her I can see the extreme devastation and exhaustion on her face. I'm not sure, but I don't think she's left my side at all. Heard Des and Jag begging her to go home take a shower and get some sleep. She refused. Taking a deep breath and blowing it out, it hits me how frigging lucky I am. This woman, no matter what I've done, has stood by my side since I was born. Contentment fills my heart and soul. Clasping her hand to get her attention, I wait for her to look up. When she does finally, I am ready to give her what she always gives me and truly mean it.

"Thanks, Mom, for loving me. I love you back, I hope you know that. None of this is because of you, I know you love me."

She stares at me with eyes that mine match. Then very slowly her lips lift into a beautiful smile.

CHAPTER THIRTY-THREE

DAISY

God, these last couple of weeks have been rough. When I finally got out of the hospital, I immediately went into outpatient therapy. I immediately started with Trinity's counselor every other week because I was referred to a crisis therapist who specializes in eating disorders for teenagers. She is blunt, takes no shit, and pushes me each and every time. I love her, which is good, because I'm going once a week to her. And finally, I'm in group therapy. This one is probably the hardest because it has opened my eyes to the fact I'm not alone. Finally grasping that is monumental or so I'm told.

When not at therapy, I'm either doing homework at home, writing in my journal, or listening to music. Music is my home therapy. I pick songs according to my moods. I've been downloading my favorite songs I find that fit a certain mood to my iPod. Currently I've put over seventy-five songs on the portable music machine.

We've talked about me going back to school and all the therapists agree that they believe I'm strong enough now. In the beginning, I couldn't even come out of my room I was so scared of my own shadow. Poor Griff kept trying, almost each day, to come over wanting to support me. Never in my wildest dreams did I think Griffin Powers would want to be my 'boyfriend.' We've talked quite a bit and he shared some of his history. He gets me better than anyone else and never pressures me for anything. I've come to depend on him, which scares the crap out of me. My regular therapist told me that's absolutely normal with dating. I snickered and rolled my eyes, so she called me on it. I tried to explain to her that we've not even been out on a real date. It was her turn to chuckle. She then explained that the definition of dating is different for each couple. She pointed out that Griff worked very hard to become my confidant and crucial in my day-to-day experiences. Once she put that out there, I realized she is absolutely right. What a blind fool I've been. I pray he continues to be a part of my life because I really like him, fingers crossed. He makes me feel protected and cherished.

So currently sitting in my room, listening to some music, as I go over my homework for the day. Remote schooling is a lot harder than I ever thought it would be. Probably because I get distracted so fast. The other day I was going over a lecture video and passed the window and spent ten or fifteen minutes watching the birds go to the feeder. *Really?* I thought to myself. Must be bored out of my mind to think watching birds was interesting. Even our cats don't watch.

Having to go to the bathroom, I put my iPod down and move my laptop and books. Walking to the bathroom, something catches my eyes. I squint to see what it is and, holy shit, is that one of my razors? Did I leave it there? When all this crap came out, the first thing Mom and Des made me do is give them my 'cutting tools.' That was so hard, felt like I was tearing a part of me off and giving it to them. And without it, in the beginning when I had a setback, I took a risk using a steak knife or scissors. Or when I was really bad, locked myself in the bathroom and used my tweezers to make the blood flow. Desperation. It's been maybe seven to ten days since I've done any of that. It's a start. Katherine, the crisis counselor in charge of my eating disorders therapy, said that in the first year or so it's going to be hard not to fall back on the cutting because its instant gratification. She explained to me the reasoning behind why people do it, and after I thought about it a bit, it made total sense. She also said that with the bingeing and purging it's an uphill battle and probably always will be.

There is no quick fix. I know that as Mom and I have had words about what I'm eating. She continues to say I eat like a bird, and I reply that I'm eating more than I have in almost a year. That shuts her up. I'm not trying to be a brat, but this isn't easy. I have stepped on a scale because I can already tell pounds are piling on.

When I spoke to Katherine about my concerns, she told me not to worry as much about what I weigh as much as how I feel. She's right, I don't get dizzy as much and the nausea is gone. Also, the metallic taste in my mouth isn't as bad as it usually was. Still losing hair, but from what I've read, that can take time, along with getting my period back. I'm taking a bunch of vitamins now due to the deficiencies my lack of eating caused.

Hearing the notification of a new text, I reach for the phone. Looking down I see it's from Griff. Opening it, he's checking on me and wants to know if I need anything. Damn, he's so nice. After I got home and settled, he came over and we talked on the back screen porch. He shared some very personal stuff with me to explain why he was in therapy. According to him, even now, if things get too much he will go talk to someone a couple times for some guidance. His honesty and sharing his secrets mean so much to me. Gives me something to work toward and I think that was his intention. Taking a minute, I text him back and ask about school, the queens, and all the new precautions in place. As we go back and forth it makes me worry about going back. But I have to because I'm just a freshman. And to get a decent job, I'm going to need a college degree.

A couple hours later, I'm lying on my bed when a knock on the door scares the heck out of me.

"Come in."

I look up just in time to see Bird and Akiria walking in, each carrying a bag. Cautiously I sit up, waiting to see what they are up to. Bird puts her bag on my bed, watching my face.

"Daisy, calm down that's your homework."

Letting my breath out, I grab the bag and look through it. Holy crap, that's a ton of homework. Oh well, something to keep my mind busy.

Turning to Akiria as she lifts her bag, placing it next to the Birdie's bag. Something is going on because I can't read either of their faces. Looking inside, I'm shocked. Inside is filled with all kinds of healthy snacks, some journal books, and a self-help workbook. I've been sharing with these two what's been going on. Akiria has been to therapy because she too has been suffering with an eating disorder. She still struggles every now and then but has come a long way. She's even started to volunteer at an animal shelter.

Tears fill my eyes at their thoughtfulness. I stand and give each of them a hug, thanking them for taking time to not only come visit me but bearing gifts. They sit on my bed and we start to catch up. I feel so removed since being in the hospital. I ask about Mary and Bird tells me she is doing better. The queens have been keeping in touch with her. Agnes's parents did a private funeral, but again the queens stepped up. Bird had her mom send flowers from all of us and then they even sent a fruit arrangement thing to the house with a poem Bird wrote from all of us about Agnes. Gotta remember before they go to get some money from Mom to pay my share.

Realizing I didn't offer them anything to drink, we

walk out to the kitchen just in time to see Jag walking in, holding his shirt in his greasy hands. Akiria freezes and Bird plows into her.

"Jesus, Kiria, watch what you're doing? Why'd you stop?"

Hearing Bird's voice, Jag raises his head taking us all in. He stops by Akiria giving her a once over head to toe, and then smiles slowly. Oh God, what a dawg my brother is.

Once he moves to wherever he was going, we sit and talk about all the gossip going on in school. I feel so out of the loop. Time flies by 'cause we are enjoying ourselves giggling, laughing, and telling stupid jokes. This is what Mom and Des walk into.

CHAPTER THIRTY-FOUR

GRIFFIN

God, I'm a fuckin' nervous wreck and don't know why. Finally got permission from Des to take Daisy out, so on the way to pick her up. Cadence, the big asshole he can be, sat me down, giving me a short talk about the birds and the bees. Then mentioned Daisy is an extension of our family and he would break my legs if I disrespect her. Before he could continue, Trinity came in giving him shit and he left me alone laughing hysterically. What a dick he can be big brother or not.

We decided to hit the aquarium 'cause we both love animals of all kinds. I haven't been there since we first moved here and my brother took me. Now he has his hands full with Hope and twins on the way.

As I stop at a light, I look to my left and, FUCK, I see Sabrina in a muscle car with some dude at the wheel. Her hands are all over as she screams like a banshee. Before I can even think to do something, he reaches over and slaps her across the face. Holy shit, what the hell is that? Light changes and he takes off like a maniac. I get behind him, figuring I can follow him to where he's heading to with that bitch. He drives like a crazy man so I continue to stay back, putting some space between our cars. Don't want to end up rear-ending this asshole. He takes a corner on two wheels and Sabrina's hands are all over as I'm sure she is screaming. Then to my shock, she reaches over and slaps the back of his head. He takes a sharp right into an empty lot and stops his car. I park on the street.

They continue arguing, I'm assuming. Then he pulls her hair, reaching beyond her, opening the passenger door. Once it is open, he pushes her out and she lands on her ass. Even from this distance I can tell she is totally pissed. Before she can say a word, he punches it and takes off to the end of the lot. Then he turns around and, oh my God, he is coming back, car aimed at Sabrina. Her back is to him as she tries to get up and when she is barely on her feet, he hits her and she goes flying. He never even looks back, just turns out of the lot. I reach for my cell, dialing 911, telling them I just witnessed an accident where someone was involved in a hit and run. They needed to get an ambulance here quickly. Glancing up, Sabrina isn't moving, so I speak to the operator as I jog over to her. I can see she is breathing shallow and there's tons of blood. I let the operator know, then kneel next to her, shoving her hair away from her face. She murmurs, "Joey," but when her eyes open and she looks directly into mine, she lets out a screech and then screams. I try to tell her to stay still but she's a feisty bitchy.

Not sure what to do, I take my hoodie off and place it gently over her to try and keep her warm. She is violently trembling so figure she is really injured and going into shock. We don't speak just stare at each other. Quite quickly I hear an ambulance approaching so I wave them in. Not wasting any time, she is placed on a backboard, neck in a brace. They do a once over and then move her right to the rig. As they place her in a cop car pulls in. The two cops approach me cautiously. They ask my name, where I live, and how or why was I here. I tell them the truth about wanting to find Joey, who is responsible for a lot of Daisy's pain and suffering. They take down my contact information and tell me not to leave the state. Like what the hell does that even mean, jerks. They inform me that this info will be shared with the detective on Daisy's case. I thank them and we part, all going to our vehicles.

Once in I reach for my phone, dialing up Jagger. I wait and it rings one, two, three times. Got voicemail. So I leave a brief message, hang up, and redial. I do this like four or five times before he picks up.

"What the fuck, asshole, ya dying?"

I actually laugh a bit then pull it together.

"No, dipshit. Found Joey. Long story short, pulled up to a light, looked to my side, and Joey and Sabrina were in apparently his muscle car. They took off fighting, exchanging blows, and when he had enough, he beat on her, opened the door, and pushed her out. Then he turned his car around and hit her head on."

Jagger makes a sound and I'm afraid to ask what that was about. He has history with this girl. She might have been his first, so gonna have a soft spot for sure.

"Is she, um, Griffin, is she dead or alive? And if she's breathing, what are they sayin'?"

Taking my time, I explain what all happened, lettin' him know I'm heading to the hospital. He says he'll meet me there after he calls the detective on the case.

Not sure if I can even check on Sabrina, but not sure if her folks are able to get there fast or even know yet. No one, even a bullying bitch like her, should be alone. I park in the emergency room area and walk in, sitting in a chair against the wall. I rest my head back. It hits me suddenly. FUCK! I was on my way to pick up Daisy. Son of a bitch. Grabbing my phone, I scroll for her digits and hit go. It rings, rings, and then goes to voicemail. I try again and leave a message. I also text her. Of course, I'm finally gonna spend quality time with my Lil' Flower so we can get to know one another, and this happens.

Hearing the sliding doors open, I look up and holy shit. Des, Jagger, Cadence, Wolf, Ugly, and Bear walk in, searching the room. Jagger sees me and points my way. I'm not a small dude but this group of guys would make anyone shit their pants. Especially with those looks on their faces. Everyone around us gets up and finds a different seat, far away from us. They all grab a seat, making themselves comfortable. Des looks my way, gives me a nod first, then starts the twenty questions.

"Griffin, did you get any information on her? How bad do you think the accident was? Was she conscious when she was brought in?"

And on and on. I figured I'd let him ramble before I even attempt to reply to the third degree he's spewing.

When he finishes and looks my way, one eyebrow raised, I just give it right back to him. To be honest, they're lucky I called them when this happened. I try to think of his first ten questions when Bear, their biker friend, chirps up with his own questions but about Joey. Like what type of car: model, make, and color. Did I see the plates? How bad was the car after he hit the female fucker?

I sit back and just wait, figuring Cadence, Wolf, and Jagger will have questions too. After about two minutes Des glares my way. I can almost see the steam coming out of his ears.

"So do you need a special invite to the party, bub? Gonna answer our questions anytime today? Believe it or not, we got shit to do. So answer Bear's first, he needs that particular info for what he's gotta do."

Recalling Bear's questions, I answer each one precisely and honestly. When I'm done Bear looks to Des, gives him a head lift, stands, and walks out without a word to anyone else with Ugly following close by. *Assholes*, I think.

Once again, I get stink eye from Des. Damn, I

thought he was a cool dude. Cadence speaks highly of him. Maybe I just rub him wrong today or he's having a bad one. Or okay, makes sense he might not like me anymore 'cause I'm interested in Daisy. Makes total sense now. So besides trying to convince Daisy, I get the pleasure of busting my ass twice with Des. Lucky fuckin' me.

CHAPTER THIRTY-FIVE

DAISY

What's the old saying, I'm all dressed up with nowhere to go? I checked my phone about ten minutes ago and saw I had a voicemail. I called and listen to Griff telling me how he happened to be in 'the right place at the wrong time.' He didn't want me to worry or think he was blowing me off. For a minute I was so mad, especially since it involves Sabrina. But if I've learned anything in counseling, it's not always about you. Got to share the floor.

So I manage to catch a ride with Des and Jagger, but when we get to the hospital I had to go use the bathroom. And as usual they were a hike down the main hall. When I finally get back and enter the emergency room, I stop dead. Holy crappity crap, why are they all here? Not because they're worried about the patient. Just when I open my mouth to ask, the doors slide open, and as I turn, the detective who took my case is walking right to Des. Well, might as well join the party.

I see the detective from the corner of my eye. She's dressed casually, but you can tell she put some effort into it. Her hair is shiny, curled at the ends. Light makeup to enhance not hide. When my eyes find hers, she gives me a 'really' look. Busted. I shift and notice Des and Wolf are spewing hate her way. I smile to myself and give them two fingers tap. They look my way and both smile immediately at me.

Sitting across from them is Jagger, who looks like crap. Wonder if he still has feelings for that twit. Then I push that thought out of my head. Two wrongs don't make a right. Mom's favorite saying. Jag stands and starts moving toward a couple who are at the desk. Must be Sabrina's parents. He waits for them to turn and when they see him, a smile appears on both of their faces. He speaks low to them, probably telling them what happened. When he points in our direction, the three of them head our way. They look normal, wonder why Sabrina is the way she is?

"Everyone, these are Sabrina's parents, Mr. and Mrs. Tolleck. That is my stepdad, Des, my sister, Daisy, and the rest our close friends, Cadence and Wolf. And that young man is Griffin. He's the one who witnessed the accident."

Both Griff and Wolf stand, offering their seats to the older couple. As they sit and start talking with Des, the guys move to the next row where they will all fit. My phone vibrates so I look at it and smile.

"Lil' Flower, why you sittin' all the way over there? I got all cleaned up for you, can't you tell? I even smell good. Come sit by me if ya want."

He's watching me read his text. Dang it, giving it all away, not holding anything close to the chest. Well, the cat's out of the bag, so I stand and walk to where he's sitting. He saved the chair next to him. When I sit, he grabs my hand, holding on, giving it a squeeze. Okay, not what we planned but we're still together. My counselors would be proud of me, finding a positive in so many negatives.

"Family for a Sabrina Tolleck. Hello, a Sabrina Tolleck.

We all turn as her parents raise their hands so the doctor walks to them. Des doesn't leave. We hear mumblings but nothing clear. I see her dad shake the doctor's hand, so she must not be too bad. A nurse is hanging back and when the man heads to the back, she tells the Tollecks she can take them up. Mr. Tolleck says something to Des, shakes his hand, and then they follow the nurse. Des comes our way.

"Well, our little troublemaker is in a world of pain right now. She has three or four fractured ribs, a shattered tibia—they are taking her to surgery to fix—bruising, and road rash. Oh, and her wrist is sprained. So she's gonna be down for quite a while."

We all look at each other after he finishes. Even though she made years of my life miserable I wouldn't wish her the hurt she's in now. Not to mention the long recovery and physical therapy. She probably won't graduate this year, unless she can manage her classes from home, if they let her. I've been out of school awhile and I struggle sometimes while she's probably looking at several weeks or even months.

Griff comes up beside me, leaning down, his voice low so only I can hear him.

"Still want to go to the aquarium or take a rain check? Your call, Lil' Flower."

With him smiling at me, holding my hand, I'd probably jump off a bridge with him.

I give it a brief thought and nod my head.

"Ya know, Griff, I'd love to go, if we still can. Haven't been anywhere for a very long time. Can't wait to see some penguins, whales, dolphins, otters, and whatever else is there. Mom told me that a beluga whale baby was recently born. I hope we can see it."

He lets my hand go and heads to Des. As he talks, I see Des's jaw tighten. Griff just keeps on going and when he is done, all my stepdad does is give a slight nod. Then he puts his hand out to shake and Des looks shocked, but lifts his hand and shakes anyway.

Griff comes back my way, smiling hugely. I look beyond him and see both Jag and Des watching us, along with Wolf. All of them have mad faces on. Cadence has both a mad look with a goofy smile on his face. Whatever. I smile at them and wave. Then my hand is grabbed and I'm being pulled out of the hospital. I smile to myself because I can't believe I'm going on a date with Griffin Powers. My luck is definitely changing fingers crossed.

CHAPTER THIRTY-SIX

JAGGER

The last two weeks shit moved pretty fast. When Sabrina was able to, after her surgery, the detectives talked to her and her parents. Being that she is seventeen, almost eighteen, if she didn't cooperate they would charge her as an adult. Later that day, Joey was picked up and charged with simple assault on Daisy, trespassing on school grounds, hit and run, and leaving the scene of an accident for what he did to Sabrina. That was gonna cost him a lot. From what Des's cop friends told him, with all these charges Joey could be looking at a long haul in jail. For what happened to Agnes, both Joey and Sabrina could be brought up on manslaughter charges. Everything is being handled by the detectives.

Daisy seems to be on the road to recovery, I pray. She goes to her different therapies every week, never missing an appointment. I see her writing in her journals and talking to both Mom and Des together and separately. She's back to hanging out with her queens. What the fuck does that even mean? And she is now seeing Griffin Powers. Des is really strict so they're lucky to be able to hit the movies or maybe go grab something to eat. Usually, they are hanging here or at the Powers' home if his Mom is there. And Des checks, believe me. My lil' sis is starting to look like herself. She's put on a couple of pounds and smiles now. She doesn't look like death warmed over. Takes showers and washes her hair regularly. Mom said one night at dinner Daisy has even been helping around the house, which of course, I get stink eye from Des. *Well, what the hell does he do around here,* I think to myself. And yeah, I'd never say that out loud. He might be getting on in age but know he can still kick my ass no doubt.

So now after Mom rode my ass, I'm in the process of cleaning my room. Fuck, I hate this shit. Who cares if dirty or clean clothes are on the floor? So it's a little dusty and I can't remember when I changed my sheets last. And on my nightstand, I empty my pockets every night so there's a ton of shit there. And I'm sure the goddamn floor is a mess, needs to be vacuumed and washed. Can't believe Des rode my ass to get this done. Whatever. It's not like I have anything planned tonight.

Grabbing all my clothes, assuming they're all dirty, I plan on putting them in my laundry basket. Washing will be another day. I'm not a fuckin' maid. My head hurts just thinking about all that needs to be done. I go to open the bathroom door and it's locked. That's weird, since Daisy's been getting help, we just let each other know when we are gonna use the bathroom. I knock and nothing. So I knock harder. I hear a faint, "Just a minute." As each minute passes I feel my anger hitting the roof.

"Daisy, what the fuck, open this door right now. DAISY."

I hear the lock open and then she is in the doorway wrapped in her robe, hair in a towel. She's looking me straight in my eyes. No fear or hiding anything. Maybe I'm wrong but was worried.

"Jag, I know you care, but please don't lose faith in me until I give you something to worry about. God, how embarrassing, but been havin' stomach issues. Mom took me to the doctor. He said from all the crap I did my gut needs time. So yeah, simply put, I can't poop. So I was in the middle of using something to help me. Okay? God, sometimes you are infuriating, Big Brother."

I watch her shaking her head and I feel like a huge ass. Before I can say anything, her stomach makes a rumbling sound. Then some gurgling noises. She grabs her stomach, turning toward the bathroom.

"Hope you don't need the bathroom, Jag, this might take a while. And know I appreciate how much you love me but, brother, I'm not a kid anymore. Got to trust me. Give me some room to breathe, if I feel like I'm falling back into my old ways I'll let you know. Okay?"

She quickly makes her way to the bathroom, turns around, and smiles at me.

"I love ya, Daisy."

"Back atcha, Jag."

Then she walks in and slams the door hard. I hear the lock engage and laugh to myself. Yeah, she's feeling better already, the lil' brat.

CHAPTER THIRTY-SEVEN

DAISY

Can't believe it, Katherine told me I can schedule my appointments every other week. That's how good I'm doing, her words not mine. And I completed the group therapy so now just the two counselors every other week. Yay me.

Not going to lie, it's a daily battle. Some days I struggle to get out of bed while others I'm like a jack-in-the-box. No one can tell me why I'm all over the board. I've done some damage to my body too with the bingeing and purging. I'm still having a hard time eating large meals or heavy foods. We are working on it though. The hardest of everything to give up is the cutting. Sometimes I miss it so much and wish I could just cut one last time. I have had a couple of setbacks in the early days, but have been good lately. Only time will tell. I'm learning how to use the tools my counselors shared with me to help when I feel like cutting. It's getting better even though I doubt it will ever go away totally.

It's been hard with the queens. I'm still close and talk to Bird and Akiria, but V and Amethyst turned on us for some reason that we still don't know. With Amethyst, she went boy crazy an got herself a 'name.' V suffered another break and has been in and out of the hospital. She just stopped talking to the three of us. We tried for a bit but even her parents seemed standoffish.

Joey was convicted and sentenced to fifteen to twenty-five years for his crimes. Most of his sentence was for hitting Sabrina and leaving. Sabrina pled down and turned against her cousin. She's currently awaiting sentencing, but will be doing some time and community service. Her parents have apologized to all of us so many times. Both of them are so ashamed at what their daughter was doing. They even started a scholarship in Agnes's name. Even Agnes's parents were shocked.

Finally, Griff is wonderful. We have gotten closer and either he's here or I go to his house. I know Des prefers us here so he can keep an eye on us. Little does he know; he has nothing to worry about. It took Griff months to give me a soft closed-mouth kiss. Actually, I'm the one pushing for more. No, not like Amethyst. I really care about Griff and we've had some deep self-reflection conversations. We've shared our dreams for the future, what's on our bucket lists, and all that crazy kind of stuff kids do when they think they're in love.

Some late nights, my heart is heavy because it took

losing a friend to realize how precious and blessed I am. Mary and I have grown super close and she's around a lot. My family and the Horde have adopted her so to speak. So whenever we are all together, Mary and her parents are now included. She's a riot and everyone loves her. We sometimes talk about Agnes and she shared in her last school she was also bullied. So the pattern was set and no one was breaking the cycle. With our bully, Sabrina, and her friends no one knows why they are like they are. The school got strict after this all came out and a bunch of them either got suspended or asked to leave the school. I feel sorry at times, but other times I think they brought it on themselves.

Hearing Jag swearing and muttering about cleaning his room I giggle. I owe Jag for my life. If he hadn't cared and paid attention, I might not be here right now. Might have gotten to the point Mary and Agnes did. My big brother has always been my guardian angel. We talked about our dad finally, or as he calls him: the sperm donor. That was hard because we are on different sides of the fence. But after we chewed the fat so to speak, I felt like a weight was lifted off my chest. Mom, Jag, and me went to my therapist so we could talk about all the crap from the past. Des even came with us once. Lots of changes, which I've been told is good.

I get up and walk into the bathroom, grab some cleaning supplies, and knock on the adjoining door. He mutters so I take that as enter. His head shoots up when he sees what's in my arms and gives me his thank God smile.

"Okay, Jag, this is how it's going to work. We are doing this together. I don't want to see your unmentionables or any pictures of naked women. You good with that, Big Brother?"

He stares at me for a minute then with a huge smile on his face walks toward me, grabbing me, pulling me in close for a hug. As I hug him back, knowing in my heart he saved my life, I hear him say softly in my ear.

"Welcome back, Daisy. Welcome back, Brat.

TOUGH SUBJECTS

Thank you for reading Daisy's Darkness. This was a very hard book to write because of the sensitive subjects that are over- whelming our young adults in today's society. I've tried to portray each subject with total honesty that my research has brought to my attention.

Please pay attention to our youth. With all that is going on in our world today we need to make sure that all children are safe.

YOUNG ADULT SUICIDE-BULLYING-SELF HARM-EATING DISORDERS

SUICIDE
SOMEONE IS FEELING HO9PELESS,
helpless/thinking of suicide To talk to someone now:
• Call **1-800-273-TALK (8255)**

- Chat with Lifeline

- Visit the National Suicide Prevention Lifeline For Spanish speakers:
- Call **1-888-628-9454**
- Visit Ayuda en Español: Lifeline

For deaf/hard of hearing:
- Call **1-800-799-4889**

Free and confidential support resources are available to you
24 hours a day, 7 days a week

BULLYING
Help Hotline **1-866-488-7386** Facts About Bullying What You Can Do

SELF HARM
If you're not sure where to turn, call the S.A.F.E. Alternatives information line.

U.S. at **1-800-366-8288** for referrals and support for cutting and self-harm.

UK: Mind Infoline – Information on self-harm and a helpline to call at 0300 123 3393 or text 86463.

Canada: Kids Help Phone – A helpline for kids and teens to call for help with any issue, including cutting and self-injury at 1-800-668-6868.

Australia: Kids Helpline – A helpline for kids and

young adults to get help with issues including cutting and self-harm. Call 1800 55 1800.

India: Helpline (India) – Provides information and support to those with mental health concerns in India. Call 1860 2662 345 or 1800 2333 330.

What is self-harm?

Self-harm can be a way of dealing with deep distress and emotional pain. It may help you express feelings you can't put into words, distract you from your life, or release emotional pain. Afterwards, you probably feel better—at least for a little while. But then the painful feelings return, and you feel the urge to hurt yourself again.

EATING DISORDERS

Contact the National Eating Disorder Association
Call-1-800-931-2237
What are Eating Disorders

ABOUT THE AUTHOR

USA Today Bestselling author D. M. Earl spins stories about real life situations with characters that are authentic, genuine and sincere. Each story allows the characters to come to life with each turn of the page while they try to find their HEA through much drama and angst.

When not writing, DM loves to read some of her favorite authors books. Also she loves to spend quality time with her hubby & family along with her 7 fur babies. When weather permits she likes to ride her Harley.

Contact D.M at DM@DMEARL.COM
Website: http://www.dmearl.com/

- facebook.com/DMEarlAuthorIndie
- twitter.com/dmearl
- instagram.com/dmearl14
- amazon.com/D-M-Earl/e/B00M2HB12U
- bookbub.com/authors/d-m-earl
- goodreads.com/dmearl
- pinterest.com/dauthor

ALSO BY D.M. EARL

DEVIL'S HANDMAIDENS MC: TIMBER-GHOST, MONTANA CHAPTER

Tink (Book #1)

GRIMM WOLVES MC SERIES

Behemoth (Book 1)

Bottom of the Chains-Prospect (Book 2)

Santa...Nope The Grimm Wolves (Book 3)

Keeping Secrets-Prospect (Book 4)

A Tormented Man's Soul: Part One (Book 5)

Triad Resumption: Part Two (Book 6)

WHEELS & HOGS SERIES

Connelly's Horde (Book 1)

Cadence Reflection (Book 2)

Gabriel's Treasure (Book 3)

Holidays with the Horde (Book 4)

My Sugar (Book 5)

Daisy's Darkness (Book 6)

THE JOURNALS TRILOGY

Anguish (Book 1)

Vengeance (Book 2)

Awakening (Book 3)

STAND ALONE TITLES

Survivor: A Salvation Society Novel

Printed in Great Britain
by Amazon